# THREADS OF REBELLION

## THREAD WITCH BOOK 2

DRAGONFIRE PRESS

# ALSO BY RICHARD FIERCE

## DRAGON RIDERS OF OSNEN

*Trial by Sorcery*
*A Bond of Flame*
*The Warrior's Call*
*The Coin of Souls*
*Wings of Terror*
*Eyes of Stone*
*Tooth and Claw*
*The Servant of Souls*
*Smoke and Shadow*
*The Dark Rider*
*The Song of Bones*
*Sword and Crown*
*Tides of Darkness*
*Wrath and Ruin*
*Tomb of Oaths*

## MARKED BY THE DRAGON

*Curse of the Dragon*
*Scale of the Dragon*
*Egg of the Dragon*
*Call of the Dragon*
*Wrath of the Dragon*
*Sacrifice of the Dragon*

# THREADS OF REBELLION

## THREAD WITCH BOOK 2

RICHARD FIERCE

Threads of Rebellion
Copyright © 2025 by Richard Fierce



Cover design by Liz Delton

Dragonfire Press

Print ISBN: 979-8-89631-090-7

To my readers.
Thank you for everything.

THREAD WITCH
2

THREADS
OF
REBELLION

RICHARD FIERCE

# CHAPTER 1
## Amara

Consciousness returned like water seeping through cracked stone—slowly, painfully. It carried with it the weight of everything she'd lost and everything she'd become. Amara's eyes opened to unfamiliar walls of weathered stone and windows thick with dust, their glass so old it warped the morning light into strange patterns that danced across her vision.

The temple had been abandoned long enough for silence to settle into its bones. No creaking floorboards from daily use, no voices calling between rooms, no familiar sounds of life. Just emptiness and stillness from a place where hope had withered and died.

She tried to sit up and immediately regretted the attempt. Her body felt like it had been taken apart and reassembled by someone who'd forgotten how the pieces were supposed to fit together. Muscles trembled with exhaustion that sleep hadn't touched, while her head pounded with a rhythm that matched her heartbeat.

But it was her arms that made her breath catch in her throat.

Thread-like scars coiled across her skin from wrist to shoulder, glowing faintly with silver light that pulsed in time with her heart. They weren't ordinary wounds—they looked like someone had stitched light itself into her flesh, creating patterns that seemed to shift and change of their own volition.

*The tapestry,* she remembered. *The souls I bound to protect us—where did they go?*

The answer came as whispers seemed to rise from her own blood, voices speaking just below the threshold of hearing. Not the gentle echoes she'd grown accustomed to from fabric and thread, but something deeper, more intimate. The souls she'd woven into her great working hadn't departed when their purpose was served—they'd taken root in her essence, becoming part of her.

*"Still here... still with you... bound by choice, not force..."*

*"Thank you... for listening... for remembering..."*

*"We chose this... chose you... don't fear us..."*

The voices carried comfort and gratitude, but their presence filled her with terror that made her hands shake. Had she saved those echoes, or enslaved them? The line between sanctuary and prison felt thinner than thread, and she was no longer certain which side of it she occupied.

Moving carefully to avoid jarring whatever new equilibrium her body had found, Amara swung her legs over the edge of the narrow stone slab and attempted to stand. The world tilted sickeningly, and she had to grip the wall to keep from collapsing as her vision grayed at the edges.

*I'm too weak,* she thought. *The weaving took too much. I'm lucky to be alive.*

But was she alive? The question felt more relevant than it should have. Her reflection in the dust-covered mirror across the room showed familiar features made strange by exhaustion and something else—an otherworldly quality that hadn't been there before, as if part of her existed in the space between life and death.

Her satchel lay on the room's single table, its contents scattered as if someone had searched through it. Among the usual scraps and threads lay her hairpin-turned-needle, but it looked different now—not steel but something that caught the light and threw it back transformed, as if the simple tool had absorbed power from contact with her gift.

She reached for it with trembling fingers, needing the familiar comfort of the instrument that had saved her life. But the moment her skin made contact with the metal, the scars along her arms flared with burning pain that made her gasp.

*Test it,* a voice whispered. It might have been her grandmother's, or it might have been her own desperate need to understand what she'd become. *See what the weaving has made of you.*

Against every instinct that screamed for caution, Amara pricked her finger with the needle's point. A single drop of blood welled up, bright red but somehow luminous, carrying light that had nothing to do with the sun streaming through the dirty windows. She pressed the bloodied finger to a scrap of cloth from her satchel and pulled a single stitch through the fabric.

The voice that escaped was sharp and clear, carrying the distinct cadence of someone she recognized—one of the royal spirits who'd supported her defiance in the Guild Hall. But instead of the gentle whisper she'd expected, the echo emerged with force that made the temple walls tremble.

*"The realm burns while cowards wear crowns. Justice delayed is justice denied. The people cry out for—"*

Amara tore the stitch free with violent haste, her heart hammering against her ribs as the voice cut off mid-sentence. The cloth crumbled to ash in her hands, while the scars along her arms pulsed with light that left afterimages burned into her vision.

Her gift was no longer separate from her body—it was in her veins, woven into her essence like thread through fabric.

The realization sent ice through her chest. She'd bound the spirits to herself so completely that they'd become part of her, their voices waiting just beneath her skin for the right stitch to set them free. Every drop of blood she shed would carry their echoes, every thread she pulled would risk unleashing memories that might be too powerful to contain.

*What have I done to myself?*

Fragments of the Guild Hall haunted her—the Pattern Council's hunger as they demanded she awaken the king's cloak, Caedric's blade flashing silver as he cut down his former colleagues, the terrible moment when she'd realized the tapestry was pulling her essence into its weave. She'd acted from desperation and defiance, not understanding the cost of binding so many souls to her own.

But had it been protection or corruption? The tapestry had shielded them from Guild authority, yes, but at what price? The voices in her blood spoke of choice, but choices made in desperation often looked different in daylight than they had in the moment of crisis.

*Where is Caedric?*

The question hit her with sudden urgency. She was alone in this abandoned place, weak as a newborn and marked with scars that proclaimed her nature to anyone with eyes to see. Without him, she felt exposed to threats from every direction—Guild hunters who would claim her abilities, cult survivors who would harvest her power, common folk who would see her as salvation... or damnation.

But even his protection raised questions that made her stomach clench with unease. He was a man who'd spent years hunting people like her, trained to see rogue weavers as threats to be eliminated. Yes, he'd chosen to protect her in the Guild Hall, but that choice had been made in the heat of battle against enemies who threatened them both.

Now, in the cold light of day, would he begin to see her as the true danger? The voices in her blood carried the wisdom and power of royal dynasties—knowledge that could reshape kingdoms if properly directed. Would Caedric's institutional training eventually override his personal loyalty?

*Can I trust him fully?*

The doubt tasted like poison, but she couldn't dismiss it. Trust was a luxury she'd never been able to afford, and her transformation had made her more valuable—and more dangerous—than ever before.

Movement outside the temple made her freeze, every muscle tensed for flight or fight despite her body's weakness. Footsteps on the overgrown path, voices speaking in hushed tones, the sound of people trying not to make noise while failing completely.

For a terrifying moment, she imagined Guild soldiers surrounding the building, their thread-cutters ready to sever the connections she'd forged with the spirits in her blood. Or Wraithstitcher survivors, their barbed needles hungry for revenge against the woman who'd destroyed their sanctuary.

Instead, when she peered through the dust-caked window, she saw a handful of villagers approaching with the careful steps of people entering a place they believed might be cursed. Common folk in rough clothing, their faces marked by the weariness that came from lives spent at the mercy of forces beyond their control.

But their eyes held recognition as they looked toward the temple, and their whispered words carried clearly in the morning air: "Thread-witch... Guild Hall... awakened the dead kings..."

*Word has already spread.*

In the time since her defiance at the Guild Hall—how long had it been? Hours? Had it possibly been days? Time felt fluid, unreliable—but stories had spread from Deymar to the surrounding settlements. Her name was probably already becoming legend, her actions transformed by repetition into something larger than the desperate gamble they'd actually been.

One of the villagers stepped forward from the group. An older man whose clothes marked him as a farmer, his hands gnarled by decades of hard work. In his arms, he carried a bundle of white cloth that made Amara's enhanced senses prickle with recognition. A wedding veil. Old, carefully preserved, heavy with memories of joy and loss.

"Please," the man called, his voice cracking with desperation. "I know you're in there, lady. I know what you can do. My wife... she passed last winter, but her veil still holds her scent. Could you... could you let me hear her voice one more time?"

Behind him, another villager hissed urgent warnings. "Don't ask her, Thomas. Thread-witches bring curses. We should leave before she notices us."

But the farmer—Thomas—ignored the advice, stepping closer to the temple with the desperate courage of someone who had nothing left to lose. "I'll pay whatever you ask. Gold, silver, my land if you want it. Just... please. I need to know she forgives me for not saving her."

The raw grief in his voice cut through Amara's defenses. This was why she'd reluctantly tried to help Selanna—not for power or glory, but to offer comfort to those who needed it most. The ability to give voice to love that death had silenced, to provide closure where none had existed before.

But now? With the spirits woven into her blood and power that threatened to consume everything it touched? The risk was too great, the potential for catastrophe too real.

More villagers were arriving, drawn by rumors and desperate hope. Some carried fabric that whispered with stored memories, others simply watched with the attention of people who believed they'd found a miracle worker. But their faces showed the same division she'd seen everywhere—fear and reverence in equal measure, terror and hope warring for dominance.

A young woman pushed through the crowd, her dress torn and muddy, her eyes wild with grief. "My baby died of the fever last month. Can you bring her back? Can you make her breathe again?"

"She's not bringing anyone back," snapped an older woman whose clothes marked her as someone with local authority, possibly a village elder. "Thread-witches steal souls. We should be driving her out, not begging for miracles."

The crowd's mood shifted like a tide turning, hope curdling into suspicion. Hands moved toward farming tools that could serve as weapons, while voices rose in argument about whether she represented salvation or damnation.

Amara pressed herself against the wall, her heart hammering as she realized the truth of her situation. She was no longer anonymous, no longer able to hide in the open. Her defiance at the Guild Hall had made her into something else entirely—a symbol that people would project their needs and fears upon regardless of her own wishes.

The sound of approaching footsteps cut through the crowd's debate. A single man, moving with the urgency of someone who knew exactly where he was going and why. Amara caught a glimpse of a black cloak and a silver blade before she saw it was Caedric, his presence immediately shifting the villagers' attention from the temple to the more immediate threat.

"Move along," he commanded. "There's nothing here for you."

"We just want to speak with her," Thomas protested, clutching his wife's veil closer to his chest. "We're not asking for anything evil, just—"

"I know what you're asking for," Caedric interrupted, his hand resting casually on his thread-cutter's hilt. "And I know what it would cost her to provide it. Move along."

The crowd hesitated, torn between desperate need and a healthy fear of Guild authority. But Caedric's reputation preceded him—even here, miles from Deymar, they knew what the black cloak represented.

Slowly, reluctantly, they began to disperse. Thomas was the last to leave, his steps dragging as he carried his wife's veil back toward the empty house awaited his return.

When the last villager had disappeared down the overgrown path, Caedric approached the temple, his steps reminding Amara of a hunter approaching a wounded animal. His pale eyes found hers through the window, and she saw relief there—not just that she was conscious, but that she was still recognizably herself.

*For now,* whispered one of the voices in her blood. *But change comes whether we choose it or not.*

As Caedric opened the door, his expression carefully neutral but his concern evident in the way he moved, Amara felt the weight of understanding settle on her shoulders like a mantle she'd never asked to wear.

The threads that bound her to the spirits in her blood, the scars that marked her transformation, the whispers that had already begun to spread—none of it cared what she'd intended when she'd woven her tapestry of defiance.

*I was never meant to be their savior,* she thought, watching hope and fear war in Caedric's eyes as he took in her transformed state. *But the threads don't care what I was meant to be.*

# CHAPTER 2
## Caedric

The forest around the abandoned temple held secrets that spoke to anyone trained to read them. Caedric moved through the underbrush with the silent efficiency of a predator, his eyes cataloguing every broken twig, every disturbed patch of earth, every sign that others had passed this way before him.

The deer trail he'd been following showed fresh hoofprints—too regular to be wild animals, too purposeful to be random travelers. Three horses, shod with iron, their riders heavy enough to leave deep impressions in the soft ground. One mount favored its left hind leg, creating a distinctive gait pattern that would be easy to track.

More concerning were the scraps of black fabric caught on thornbushes along the path. Not the rough cloth of common travelers, but the fine weave of Guild uniforms, torn during hasty passage through the dense woods. The threads still held traces of the silver sigils that marked Hemlock Circle authority, their power dimmed but recognizable to someone who'd worn such fabric for years.

*They're close,* Caedric thought, his hand moving instinctively to the thread-cutter at his belt. *Closer than I'd hoped.*

The Guild's hunters had been his brothers-in-arms once, men he'd trained beside and trusted with his life during countless dangerous missions. They knew his techniques as well as he knew theirs, understood his tactical thinking because they'd learned from the same instructors. Facing them would be like cutting apart pieces of his own identity, destroying bonds forged in blood and shared purpose.

But those bonds had been based on lies, he reminded himself. Service to an institution that fed prisoners to cultists while maintaining facades of righteousness. Loyalty to authorities who saw people like Amara as resources to be claimed rather than individuals with rights and dignity.

The initiation ceremony haunted his memory as he picked his way through thorny undergrowth—kneeling before the Pattern Council while Needlewarden Korren wrapped silver thread around his forearm, the binding tight enough to draw blood. *"By thread and blade, I swear to unmake what should never be,"* he'd recited along with the other initiates, their voices raised in unison. *"To serve the realm's stability above all personal desire."*

The thread had been more than symbolic. Guild weavers had worked power into its fibers, creating a connection that would alert the Council if their agents ever betrayed their oaths. Even now, miles from Deymar and officially declared a traitor, Caedric could feel that silver strand tugging at his consciousness like a fishhook lodged in his soul.

It should have been agony, the binding fighting against his rebellion. Instead, it felt... loose, somehow. As if the connections that had once seemed unbreakable were fraying under the weight of truths the Guild couldn't deny.

*Perhaps loyalty to Amara is the truer oath,* he thought, stepping carefully around a patch of ground that showed recent disturbance. *Perhaps protecting the innocent matters more than serving corrupt authority.*

The temple came into view through the trees, its weathered walls looking fragile in the morning light. But the scene unfolding in its overgrown yard made Caedric's blood run cold—villagers surrounding the building, their voices raised in desperate pleading and fearful accusation.

He'd left Amara alone for three hours, scouting the area and checking the snares he'd set for rabbits. Long enough for word to spread from settlement to settlement, carrying tales of the thread-witch who'd defied the Guild and awakened the dead. Long enough for desperation to overcome common sense and drive people to seek miracles they couldn't afford.

These were common folk—farmers and tradesmen. They scattered before his advance like leaves before wind, their need for hope no match for their fear of Guild retribution.

Only one man hesitated—an older farmer clutching a bundle of white cloth with the desperate grip of someone holding his last connection to happiness. A wedding veil.

"Move along," Caedric commanded, letting authority ring in his voice. "There's nothing here for you."

"We just want to speak with her," the man said, pressing the gossamer fabric against his heart. "We're not asking for anything evil, just—"

"I know what you're asking for. And I know what it would cost her to provide it. Move along."

The farmer's shoulders sagged with defeat, but he obeyed. They all surrendered in the end, their footsteps heavy as they retreated to their homes and lives that no seamstress could mend.

When the last villager had disappeared down the forest path, Caedric approached the temple. Through the dusty window, he could see Amara watching him, her face pale with exhaustion.

The scars along her arms glowed faintly through her torn sleeves, thread-like patterns that pulsed with their own internal light. Whatever had happened during her working in the Guild Hall, it had changed her on a fundamental level. The spirits she'd bound hadn't simply served her purpose and departed—they'd taken root in her, becoming part of whatever she was evolving into.

For a moment, seeing the terror and shame in her gold-flecked eyes, Caedric felt his carefully maintained emotional distance begin to crack. She'd sacrificed everything to protect souls the Guild would have enslaved, and now she was paying the price in ways he didn't fully understand.

He wanted to offer comfort, to tell her that transformation didn't have to mean corruption, that power could be controlled and directed toward worthy purposes. But the words felt inadequate against the magnitude of what she faced.

Instead, he forced his expression back to neutral professionalism. *Distance serves her better than sympathy,* he told himself. *She needs a protector, not another person seeking pieces of her soul.*

Inside the temple, his eyes swept the chamber like a merchant tallying wares, calculating what they had against what they would need in the days ahead. Food supplies: enough dried meat and hardtack for perhaps three days, assuming careful rationing. Water: a well behind the building that still ran clear, though its depth was uncertain. Shelter: adequate for now, but the building's isolation worked against them as much as it protected them.

Most concerning was their complete lack of allies. No safe houses to retreat to, no network of supporters who might offer aid, no resources beyond what they carried and what they could scavenge. The Guild's reach extended across every kingdom in the realm, while the Wraithstitchers operated in the shadows that touched every settlement.

*Running will not be enough,* Caedric realized with growing certainty. *Sooner or later, we'll be cornered. The question is whether she'll be ready when that happens.*

He could keep her hidden like prey, moving from one temporary shelter to another until exhaustion or bad luck delivered them to their enemies. Or he could teach her to fight like a soldier, to use her transformed abilities as weapons rather than burdens.

The choice would determine not just their survival, but what kind of people they became in the process.

While Amara rested, Caedric made another circuit of the surrounding forest, checking the rabbit snares he'd set at dawn. The small game was essential—they couldn't risk approaching settlements for supplies, not when every stranger might recognize Amara.

It was while examining tracks near the creek that fed the temple well that he found it: a symbol carved into the bark of an ancient oak, the cuts fresh enough that sap still wept from the wounds.

A crooked spindle wrapped in thread, the mark twisted until it resembled a spider in its web.

The Wraithstitchers' sign, left by scouts to mark territory and communicate with other cult members. They weren't just hunting Amara—they were mapping the area, establishing escape routes and ambush points, preparing for a coordinated strike.

But why leave such an obvious sign? The cultists he'd fought in Deymar's catacombs had been subtle predators, patient and careful in their approach. This felt different, almost deliberately provocative.

*They're not just chasing her,* he realized with growing dread. *They're hunting in plain sight. They're growing bolder.*

The rabbit in his snare hung limp and still, its neck cleanly broken by the wire trap. Caedric removed it with mechanical efficiency, but his mind was already racing through possibilities. How many cultists were operating in the area? What resources did they have access to? How much time remained before they felt confident enough to strike?

More importantly, should he tell Amara what he'd discovered?

The argument for honesty was clear—she deserved to know the scope of the threat they faced, deserved the chance to prepare herself mentally and physically for what was coming. But she was already struggling. Adding the immediate pressure of cult surveillance might shatter whatever fragile stability she'd achieved.

*Information can be a weapon pointed in either direction,* he thought, securing the rabbit to his belt and beginning the walk back to the temple. *Sometimes ignorance serves better than knowledge.*

The decision felt like another small betrayal, another step away from the partnership they'd begun to build in the Guild Hall's ruins. But protection sometimes required difficult choices, sacrificing comfort for safety even when the protected person couldn't understand or appreciate the necessity.

Amara was sitting by one of the temple's windows when he returned, her needle gleaming in her lap but her hands carefully folded away from its silver surface. She looked up as he entered, and he saw questions in her eyes that he wasn't ready to answer.

"The villagers won't return," he said instead, hanging the rabbit from a hook near the cold fireplace. "Word will spread that this place is watched by Guild authority. That should buy us some time."

"Time for what?" she asked quietly.

Her words hung between them like a thread pulled taut, waiting for the snip of his answer. Time to heal? Time to plan? Time to become something other than what they were now? Caedric wasn't sure he had answers to any of those possibilities.

"Time to decide what comes next," he said finally.

Privately, his vow was clearer than any words he could speak aloud. The Guild could send their hunting parties, the Wraithstitchers could weave their nets, the whole kingdom could line up to claim pieces of her soul. They would find him standing in the way, a barrier between Amara and everyone that would seek to use or destroy her.

Caedric was no longer an Unraveler of the Guild. He was Amara's shield.

# CHAPTER 3
## Amara

"We need supplies," Amara said, pulling her torn cloak tighter around her shoulders that still ached from the scars coiling beneath the fabric. "Food, clean water, thread for mending. We can't survive on what little we have."

Caedric looked up from where he crouched beside the temple well, his pale eyes reflecting the quiet assessment she'd grown accustomed to over their days in hiding. "It's too dangerous. The villages will be watching for us."

"Then we'll be careful. Keep our heads down, buy what we need, leave quickly." She gestured toward their meager supplies— barely enough dried meat for another day, water that tasted of rust from the old well, clothing that grew more ragged by the day. "We can't live like hunted animals forever."

Something flickered across his expression—doubt, perhaps, or recognition that her logic was sound despite the risks. They'd been subsisting on what he could catch in his snares and what edible plants they could identify, but winter was coming and the forest's bounty wouldn't last forever.

"Stay close," he said finally. "Let me do the talking. And if anything feels wrong—anything at all—we leave immediately."

The village of Millhaven nestled against the banks of a stream that whispered of its past glory days turning mill wheels, the village's ancient cobblestones polished to a dull sheen by centuries of wooden carts and farmers' boots. Market day brought farmers from surrounding settlements, their stalls heavy with the last harvest before winter's grip tightened on the land.

But something felt different the moment they entered the square. Conversations didn't simply pause when Amara passed—they died entirely. Eyes lingered too long on her face, mothers pulled their children closer, and whispers rose in her wake.

*"Thread-witch..."*

*"...defied the Guild..."*

*"...awakened the dead kings themselves..."*

The rumors had spread faster than she'd imagined possible. In the week since their escape from Deymar, stories had transformed her desperate gamble in the Guild Hall into something larger, something far more legendary. She was no longer just a rogue weaver on the run—she'd become a symbol that people projected their hopes and fears upon.

At the baker's stall, the merchant refused to meet her eyes. "Sorry, miss. Fresh out of everything you might want." His lie was obvious as loaves of bread sat in plain sight behind him.

"I have coin," Amara said quietly, placing silver pieces on his counter.

"Guild's got long reach," the baker muttered, not touching the money. "Don't need their attention on my family. Best you move along."

But even as one merchant turned her away, another pressed forward from the crowd. An older man with calloused hands and desperate eyes, clutching a piece of faded fabric that made Amara's enhanced senses prickle with recognition.

"Please," he whispered urgently, thrusting the cloth toward her. "My son died at harvest time. Fever took him quick, but this kerchief was his favorite. He used it to wipe his nose when he cried. Could you... could you let me hear his voice one more time?"

The kerchief the moment it touched her palm, memory jolting into her like a current rather than a whisper. This was no faint echo but a desperate plea, scratching at the walls of her mind like someone trapped behind a door, pounding to be let in. The voices in her blood responded immediately, stirring with recognition and hunger.

*"Papa? Papa, why are you crying?"*

The words formed without her conscious direction, spilling from the fabric like water from a broken dam. The child's voice was bright with confusion and love, carrying the cadence of someone too young to understand why the adults around him looked so sad.

Amara jerked her hand back as if the cloth had burned her, but the damage was done. The man's face crumpled with joy and anguish, while other villagers pressed closer with their own precious scraps of memory.

"My daughter's dress—"

"My husband's gloves—"

"My mother's wedding ring—"

The crowd surged forward, and Amara felt the scars along her arms begin to burn. Each piece of fabric they thrust toward her carried its own echoes, its own whispers demanding acknowledgment. The voices in her blood rose in response, eager to bridge the gap between living grief and remembered love.

*Control,* she told herself desperately. *You have to maintain control.*

But control felt like trying to dam a flooding river with her bare hands. The more she fought against her gift's response to so much sorrow, the stronger it became. Power that had once required conscious effort now stirred with every heartbeat, every breath, every moment of contact with fabric that held human memory.

A child broke free from her mother's grip, running toward Amara with fearless curiosity. She carried a rag doll, its button eyes loose and its fabric body worn smooth by countless nights of being held close.

"Lady, lady!" the child called, pressing the doll into Amara's hands before her mother could intervene. "Can you make Rosie talk? She used to tell me stories, but now she's quiet."

The moment the doll touched her skin, power erupted beyond her ability to contain it. The child's echo burst free with startling clarity—a high-pitched giggle followed by words that carried the pure joy of innocent play.

*"Mama! Come play with us! Rosie says she knows a new song!"*

The market square fell silent as if sound itself had been cut away with a blade. Some villagers gasped in awe, others stepped back in terror, but all of them stared at the woman whose arms glowed with thread-like scars while a dead child's laughter echoed from a simple cloth doll.

*This is what they see,* Amara realized with growing horror. *Not a person struggling with unwanted power, but a monster who plays with the voices of the dead.*

She dropped the doll and stumbled backward, but the damage was spreading. Other fabrics in the market began to whisper in response to her lost control—merchant's aprons, children's clothing, the worn cloaks of elderly villagers. Decades of stored memory stirred toward wakefulness, threatening to transform the entire square into a chorus of the departed.

Caedric's hand closed around her wrist with gentle firmness, his presence a solid anchor in the storm of voices threatening to overwhelm her consciousness. "We're leaving. Now."

He guided her through the crowd, his free hand resting on his thread-cutter's hilt in a gesture that discouraged pursuit. But Amara could feel the stares following them, could hear the whispers that would spread from this village to the next until her name became legend across every settlement in the realm.

They walked in tense silence until the village walls disappeared behind trees, the market's chaos fading to memory. Only then did Amara's carefully maintained composure finally crack.

"You dragged me away like a prisoner," she said, rounding on Caedric with the fury that had been building since the moment he'd taken her wrist. "Like I was some dangerous animal that needed restraining."

"You were losing control," he replied with a calmness that infuriated her more than if he'd shouted. "Another moment and you would have awakened every scrap of fabric in the square. The panic alone could have gotten people killed."

"I can't keep hiding—but I can't even hold a piece of cloth without it screaming at me." The words came out broken, carrying all the fear and frustration she'd been suppressing since awakening with voices in her blood. "Every thread remembers. Every piece of fabric wants to speak. How am I supposed to live like this?"

"You need to learn to control it… before it kills you. Or someone else."

The blunt honesty of his words hit like a physical blow. But beneath his harsh assessment, she caught something else—not condemnation, but recognition. He understood the weight she carried, the impossible balance between power and responsibility that threatened to crush her if she faltered.

"And if I can't?" she asked quietly.

"Then we'll face that problem when it comes. But not today." His eyes held hers. "You're stronger than this. Stronger than the voices, stronger than the fear. You just need to remember that strength when the voices get loud."

For a moment, the professional distance he maintained wavered, revealing glimpses of the man beneath the protector's mask. Someone who'd chosen her over everything he'd built his identity around, who'd abandoned institutional loyalty for the sake of someone he barely knew.

*We're bound together by this,* she realized. *Neither of us can go back to what we were before.*

As they were leaving the last farmhouses on the outskirts of the village, movement caught her attention. A cloaked figure. Their presence was different from the common folk they'd encountered in the market. Not threatening, exactly, but deliberate in a way that made her enhanced senses prickle with awareness.

The stranger raised one hand in what might have been a greeting or a farewell, and words carried on the wind despite the distance between them.

"Threads remember. We can teach you to listen."

Before Amara could respond, the figure retreated, leaving her with questions that had no easy answers. Who were "we"? What kind of teaching did they offer? And why did the words feel less like a threat and more of an offer?

⸻◆⸻

That night, camped in a grove of ancient oaks near the temple, Amara sat beside their small fire and stared at the scars that coiled along her arms. In the flickering light, they seemed to move with their own rhythm, pulsing in time with heartbeats that might have been hers or might have belonged to the spirits woven into her blood.

The voices whispered constantly now. They didn't demand attention, but were simply present, like background music that had become so familiar she barely noticed it unless she concentrated. Royal wisdom and common love, soldier's courage and child's innocence, all of it bound to her essence.

*If I don't master this,* she thought, watching shadows dance across fabric that glowed with its own internal light, *I will become the monster they already see.*

But mastery required understanding, and understanding required guidance from someone who'd walked this path before. The stranger's words echoed in her memory: *We can teach you to listen.*

Perhaps salvation lay not in fighting the voices, but in learning to hear them properly.

Perhaps control came not from suppression, but from a partnership with the spirits that had chosen to bind themselves to her fate.

The questions would have to wait for daylight and whatever answers tomorrow might bring. But for the first time since awakening with thread-like scars, Amara felt something that might have been hope stirring beneath the fear.

She wasn't alone in this transformation. Somewhere in the realm, others existed who understood the weight of voices in her blood, the responsibility of speaking for the dead. And if they could teach her to master what she'd become, perhaps she could transform from a monster into something else entirely.

The fire crackled and sparked, sending embers toward the stars. In the distance, wolves howled their lonely songs, while closer by, Caedric kept watch with the steady vigilance of someone who'd made her safety his sacred duty.

*Tomorrow,* she promised the voices in her blood. *Tomorrow we'll find answers.*

# CHAPTER 4
## Caedric

Caedric crouched beside a muddy stream crossing, studying the impressions left by boots that had passed this way perhaps hours before them. Four men, moving with the heavy-footed confidence of people who weren't concerned about stealth. One favored his right leg, creating a distinctive drag pattern. Another wore boots with a nail missing from the left heel, leaving characteristic marks in the soft earth.

They made no effort to mask their trail, no attempt to move silently through the undergrowth. These weren't Guild Unravelers, who moved through hostile territory like smoke. These were common mercenaries, armed and dangerous but lacking the skill that marked his former brothers-in-arms.

*The Guild has sent outsiders,* he realized with growing unease. *Keeping their own hands clean while others do the hunting.*

But that didn't explain the previous signs he'd found indicating the Hemlock Circle was in the area. Further along the trail, he found more evidence of their passage. A campfire hastily extinguished but still warm enough to raise steam when he poured water on the ashes. Scraps of food that came from provisions rather than the land. Horse dung fresh enough to buzz with flies, indicating mounts hobbled nearby while their riders scouted on foot.

They were close. Too close.

Caedric backtracked toward where he'd left Amara resting beside a granite outcropping, but the sound of voices through the trees made him freeze. Not her voice— rough, male tones. He moved through the underbrush with the silent efficiency of a predator, years of training allowing him to approach without disturbing so much as a fallen leaf.

Through a gap in the foliage, he could see them clearly: four mercenaries in leather armor, their weapons well-maintained but unremarkable. Common steel rather than the enchanted blades the Guild provided its elite agents.

But their other equipment told a different story. Each man wore a cloak that seemed to absorb light rather than reflect it, the fabric worked with threads that made him recoil. Null-thread—woven material designed to dampen supernatural manifestations, to create dead zones where magic simply failed to function.

Such fabric was Guild property, jealously guarded and never shared with outsiders. The fact that common mercenaries carried it meant Guild corruption had reached levels he'd never imagined possible.

"—the witch and the traitor," one of them was saying, his voice carrying through the undergrowth. "Alive if possible, but dead if necessary. Triple payment if we bring the Guild her needle."

"What's so special about a seamstress?" asked another, younger by his voice and apparently less experienced.

"Not just any seamstress. This one's got blood that sings, they say. Can wake the dead with nothing but thread and will." The leader's laugh held no warmth. "Guild wants to study how she does it, maybe train others to copy her techniques."

Caedric's grip tightened on his thread-cutter as understanding dawned. They weren't hunting Amara for justice or even revenge—they wanted to dissect her abilities, to understand the process that had bound spirits to her blood so they could replicate it in more controllable subjects.

"And the traitor?" the young mercenary asked.

"Used to be Hemlock Circle, they say. Went soft, chose her over his oath." The leader spat into the undergrowth. "Guild wants him alive for questioning, but I say a dead traitor sends a better message than a living one."

The casual dismissal of his life should have stung, but Caedric felt only cold calculation. Four men, armed with conventional weapons but protected by null-thread that would neutralize some of his advantages. They were positioned between him and Amara's resting place, close enough that any sound of combat would draw her into danger.

They continued discussing their plans instead of implementing them, giving him time to prepare while they revealed their intentions. Caedric had intended to circle around their position, to warn Amara and organize a tactical withdrawal before the mercenaries realized they'd been discovered. But as he moved through the trees, his foot slipped on a rock that shifted under his weight, the sound carrying clearly in the quiet of the woods.

"There!" The leader shouted. "In the trees! Take him alive if you can!"

They moved with competence, fanning out to cut off escape routes while maintaining their formation. Not Guild-trained, but experienced enough to coordinate their assault without verbal commands. The null-thread cloaks billowed around them, creating zones of supernatural silence that made his skin crawl.

Caedric's thread-cutter sang from its sheath as he met their charge. His years of Guild training had honed him into a weapon designed specifically for supernatural combat, but these men fought with the dirty pragmatism of people who killed for coin rather than principle.

The first mercenary came at him with a sword aimed at his throat, but Caedric's blade was already in motion, cutting through the man's guard to find the gap between armor plates. Blood sprayed in an arc as the mercenary stumbled backward, his weapon dropping from nerveless fingers.

But the null-thread cloak around his shoulders absorbed the supernatural edge of Caedric's strike, turning what should have been a killing blow into merely a serious wound. The man staggered but remained upright, reaching for a backup weapon.

*They're protected,* Caedric realized with growing alarm. *The cloaks don't just dampen magic—they provide actual defense.*

The second attacker tried to flank him while he was engaged with the first, but Caedric spun with fluid grace, his blade unleashing a silver arc that caught the man across the ribs. Again, the null-thread absorbed most of the impact, though enough force remained to send the mercenary reeling.

Behind him, he heard Amara's voice. She'd been drawn into the fight despite his efforts to keep her clear, forced to defend herself with abilities that grew more unstable under pressure. Light flared through the trees as spectral defenders materialized around her position. The scars along her arms blazed with silver fire, visible even through the fabric of her sleeves.

*She's losing control again,* Caedric thought, parrying a thrust aimed at his heart. *The stress is making her gift react without conscious direction.*

The tide of battle turned when Amara's defenders reached the mercenaries' position. Ghostly hands passed through null-thread protection as if it didn't exist, grasping at souls rather than flesh, disrupting the coordination that had made the hired killers dangerous.

But the effort was draining her. Caedric could see her swaying on her feet, blood streaming from her nose as the spirits in her blood answered her call for aid. Each manifestation demanded payment in essence she could barely afford to spend.

"Retreat!" he called, grabbing her arm and pulling her toward the deeper forest. "We're leaving!"

They fled through undergrowth that tore at their clothes and scratched their skin, the sound of pursuit echoing behind them like hunting calls. But the mercenaries' heavy armor worked against them in the dense woodland, while Caedric's knowledge of wilderness survival gave him advantages that gold couldn't purchase.

By the time darkness fell, they'd put enough distance between themselves and their hunters to risk a small fire hidden in a rocky depression. Amara sat hunched beside the flames, her face pale with exhaustion, her hands trembling as she tried to thread a needle for basic repairs to her torn clothing.

"If the Guild arms mercenaries like that," she said quietly, "the whole kingdom will turn against us. There'll be no safe haven anywhere in the realm."

Her words rang with a truth he couldn't deny. Null-thread cloaks represented resources that only the Guild could provide, which meant the Guild had reached the point where they were willing to arm common criminals with tools once reserved for their elite agents.

*How many mercenary bands have they equipped?* Caedric wondered. *How far does their reach extend?*

"You're bleeding," he said, noticing the dark stains on her sleeves where the scars had flared brightest during combat.

She pulled back when he reached toward her, her eyes flashing with something that might have been anger or hurt. "You treat me like a soldier under your command, not a partner. Give orders, expect obedience, make decisions without consultation."

The accusation stung, but she was right. As an Unraveler, he'd often fought alone—his blade and oath sufficient for any challenge the Guild assigned. But with Amara, protection required different strategies, demanded his trust in abilities he didn't fully understand.

"I'm trying to keep you alive," he said finally.

"I know. But keeping me alive isn't the same as keeping me human." Her voice revealed her weariness. "Every time you make a choice for me, every time you decide what's best without asking, you make me a little less of a person and a little more of a responsibility."

The words hit harder than any mercenary's blade. He'd been protecting her as if she were a valuable object rather than an individual with agency and will, making decisions based on his assessment of threats rather than her expressed needs or desires.

*Trust means risk,* he realized. *But without trust, protection becomes another form of prison.*

While Amara slept fitfully beside the dying fire, Caedric examined one of the null-thread cloaks they'd taken from the mercenaries. The fabric reeked of Guild craftsmanship—silver threads worked into patterns he recognized from his training, sigils that required master weavers to create and substantial resources to maintain.

This wasn't just corruption, it was desperation. The Guild was willing to arm common criminals with their most guarded secrets, to sacrifice principles that had guided them for centuries, all for the chance to claim one rogue weaver whose abilities threatened their monopoly on magical practice.

*They're not hunting her in secret anymore,* he thought, watching flames dance across the fabric that absorbed light like a living thing. *They're hunting her with the kingdom's coin, using the realm's own resources to fund their obsession.*

The implications were staggering. If the Guild would hire mercenaries, what other compromises had they made? How many innocent people would suffer because they had chosen power over principle?

But more immediately, if they were willing to go this far, what limits remained on their methods? Would they arm cultists next, providing Wraithstitchers with Guild resources? Would they poison wells, burn villages, turn the entire realm into a hunting ground for one woman whose only crime was using forbidden power to free tortured souls?

*If the Guild will corrupt even common men to catch her,* Caedric thought, his hand moving to the thread-cutter at his belt, *then there is no one left to trust but me.*

The weight of that responsibility settled on his shoulders like a cloak made of lead. Not just her physical safety, but her humanity, her agency, her right to choose her own path rather than submit to those who would claim ownership of her gift.

He was all that stood between Amara and forces that saw her as prize to be won rather than a person to be protected. The Guild, the cultists, the growing legend among the common folk that transformed her into a symbol rather than an individual—all of them wanted pieces of her soul, and all of them would take what they wanted whether she consented or not.

But consent mattered. Choice mattered. And if he was truly committed to protecting her, he had to protect her right to make her own decisions even when those decisions increased the danger they both faced.

*Tomorrow,* he promised silently, watching her sleep while spirits whispered in her blood and power pulsed through the scars that marked her transformation. *Tomorrow I'll ask instead of assuming. Trust instead of commanding. Treat her like the partner she wants to be rather than the responsibility I've made her into.*

In the distance, wolves howled, while closer by, the null-thread cloak continued its unnatural absorption of light and warmth. But beneath it all, barely audible even to his enhanced hearing, came the sound of Amara's quiet breathing. It was steady, peaceful even.

She was stronger than the voices, stronger than the fear, stronger than the forces arrayed against them both. He just needed to remember that strength when his protective instincts urged him to treat her like something fragile rather than someone formidable.

The real battle, he was beginning to understand, wasn't against external enemies. It was against the assumption that protection required control, that love demanded obedience, that keeping someone safe meant keeping them small.

If they were going to survive what was coming, it needed to be as equals. As partners.

As two people who'd chosen each other over everything else the world had to offer.

Anything less would be just another form of the corruption they fought against.

# CHAPTER 5
## Amara

The ruins crouched against the hillside like the bones of some ancient giant, their weathered stones overgrown with moss and trailing vines. What had once been walls now stood in broken fragments, their surfaces carved with patterns—needles and threads worked into stone with such skill that they seemed to move in Amara's periphery.

"This was a weaver's hall," Amara said, running her fingers along symbols that felt warm despite the morning chill. "They're old. Older than the Guild, I think."

Caedric studied the ruins without emotion, but she could see unease in the set of his shoulders. "The stones feel... odd. Like they're waiting for something."

He was right. The air itself hummed with anticipation, carrying whispers just below the threshold of hearing. They weren't like the whispers from fabric, but something deeper, as if the very stones were speaking.

They'd fled through the night after escaping the mercenaries, following deer paths and stream beds that left minimal trail for pursuit. But exhaustion had finally forced them to seek shelter, and the ruins offered protection from both weather and watching eyes.

*If we can stand the watching stones,* Amara thought, noting how the carved symbols seemed to track her movement across the courtyard.

She should have been more cautious. The warning signs were there —a prickling along her spine, the sudden silence of birds, the way shadows seemed to linger where no shadow should be —all the markers of a place where magic had settled like sediment, hardening into something both beautiful and deadly. But something about the ruins called to her with the same insistence as the voices in her blood.

While Caedric secured their perimeter, Amara found herself drawn deeper into the complex. A half-collapsed corridor led toward what might have been the hall's heart, its ceiling open to the sky but its walls still bearing traces of magnificent craftsmanship.

The chamber beyond took her breath away.

It dominated the space like an altar dedicated to forces beyond mortal understanding—a massive stone beam that had once been part of a loom larger than any she'd ever imagined. The fragment stood upright despite its enormous weight, its surface carved with sigils that pulsed with faint light, threaded through with veins of crystal that glowed like captured starlight.

*The Loom,* whispered voices that might have been her own thoughts or might have come from the stones themselves. *The first and greatest working, the frame that holds all threads in place.*

Her hands moved toward the fragment without conscious direction, drawn by forces she couldn't name or resist. The moment her fingertips touched the warm stone, power exploded through her consciousness like lightning.

The scars along her arms blazed with silver fire as every spirit bound to her blood responded to the proximity with something that shared their nature. But this wasn't the chaotic awakening she'd experienced in the market. This was harmony, recognition, the sound of instruments finding their proper key.

Whispers rose around her, louder than ever, chanting words that vibrated the air like plucked harp strings.

*"Threadbearer... Unraveling... Loom..."*

And then the vision took her.

She stood in a world that existed before kingdoms, before the Guild, before the careful divisions that separated one thread from another. Ancient weavers moved through landscapes that were more idea than substance, their needles pulling meaning from chaos, binding sky to stone and sea to shore with threads of pure intention.

They were giants, these first practitioners, their understanding encompassing forces that modern weavers couldn't even name. She watched them shape mountains with careful stitches, guide rivers through valleys with threads strong as steel, weave the very concept of seasons into patterns that would endure until time itself unraveled.

At the center of their great working stood the Loom—not stone and wood, but crystallized possibility, the framework that held reality itself in stable configuration. Every thread in creation passed through its frame, every pattern found its place within its vast design.

But then came the cutting.

The vision shifted, showing her Guild founders in their first incarnation—not the corrupt institution she knew, but earnest practitioners who believed power required strict control. She watched them approach the Loom with silver blades designed to sever threads they deemed dangerous, to claim authority over weaving that had once been free to all who possessed the gift.

*They meant well,* she realized with horror. *They thought they were protecting the world from chaos.*

Instead, they'd created the very chaos they feared. Each cut thread snapped back into the Loom's frame, creating tension that built over centuries like pressure in a kettle. The great working that had once been seamless began to show stress fractures, reality itself developing weak points where the original patterns had been disrupted.

And then she saw the tear.

It spread through the Loom like an infection through healthy flesh each thread dissolving into nothingness where the corruption touched it, leaving behind only absence where the warp and weft had sung with memory and light.

The vision's final revelation unfolded with the force of a thunderclap: herself standing at the center of the damaged Loom, needle in hand, surrounded by figures in Guild black and cultist white. Both sides reaching toward her with desperate hunger, both convinced that her power was the key to either repairing or completing the great unraveling.

But in the vision, she held something else—not just her simple steel needle, but understanding. Knowledge of what the Loom had been before the cutting, what it could become if the patterns were rewoven with wisdom instead of fear.

*Choice,* whispered the voices in her blood. *Everything depends on choice.*

The vision ended as abruptly as it had begun, leaving Amara gasping on the chamber floor while blood dripped from her nose onto the stones beneath her. Her bones had become strangers to her muscles, her skin a garment sewn too tight in some places and too loose in others—recognizable but fundamentally changed.

"Amara!" Caedric's voice carried panic and fury in equal measure as he knelt beside her, his hands checking for injuries while his eyes blazed with anger. "What did you do? I told you to stay close!"

She tried to speak, but words felt inadequate to contain what she'd witnessed. The scope of it—not just her personal transformation, but the cosmic implications of threads that bound reality itself. The responsibility that came with understanding how fragile the patterns truly were.

"It knows me," she whispered finally, her voice barely audible even to herself. "The Loom... it knows me."

His pale eyes searched her face, looking for signs of the madness that sometimes claimed those who touched power beyond mortal comprehension. But she felt more lucid than she had since awakening with voices in her blood, clarity cutting through confusion like her needle through cloth.

"We're leaving," he said, his tone making it obvious he expected no resistance. "Now. Before whatever's in that thing decides to take more than blood."

The familiar pattern of command and expected obedience sent anger flashing through her exhaustion. "You don't understand what I saw—"

"I understand that you're bleeding from places blood shouldn't come from. I understand that thing nearly killed you just from touching it." His grip on her arm was gentle but firm, designed to help her stand whether she wanted to or not. "And I understand that the Guild would massacre entire villages for the chance to control something like this."

"Maybe they're right to want it," she said, pulling free of his assistance despite the way the chamber spun around her. "Maybe this is bigger than what we want or fear."

"Nothing is bigger than keeping you alive." The words scraped from his throat like steel across stone, his usual mask of detached professionalism cracking to reveal something raw and unguarded. "Nothing is worth losing you to some ancient power."

She wanted to explain that it wasn't like that, that the Loom fragment had shown her recognition rather than hunger, understanding rather than exploitation. But the words felt too large for her throat, as if human speech itself had never evolved to carry the weight of what she'd just witnessed.

Instead, she let him guide her away from the chamber, away from the fragment that still called to her with harmonies that made her scars sing in response. But with each step toward the ruins' exit, the weight of what she'd witnessed grew heavier rather than lighter.

*I am not running from this,* she thought, casting one last look back at the corridor. *If the world itself is stitched together, if reality depends on patterns that are failing, then I must learn to hold the needle—or watch it all unravel.*

The voices in her blood whispered agreement. They understood what Caedric couldn't yet see—that some responsibilities transcended personal safety, that some knowledge demanded action regardless of cost.

The Guild saw her as a resource to be claimed. The Wraithstitchers saw her as power to be harvested. But the Loom saw her as something else entirely—a threadbearer, someone capable of holding patterns together even when everything else fell apart.

Whether she was strong enough for that responsibility remained to be seen. But as they left the ruins behind and returned to their endless flight through hostile territory, Amara felt something she hadn't experienced since awakening with transformed abilities.

Purpose. Not the desperate survival that had driven her since escaping Deymar, but genuine understanding of why her gift had evolved as it had, why the spirits had chosen to bind themselves to her essence.

The world was unraveling. It had been unraveling for centuries, so slowly that most people never noticed the threads pulling loose around them. But she could see it now, could feel it in every whisper that rose from fabric and stone.

And perhaps, if she was willing to pay the price, she could do something about it.

*I will learn,* she promised the voices in her blood as they made camp among the trees. *I will learn what it truly means to be a threadbearer.*

Behind them, hidden by distance and intervening hills, the loom fragment continued its patient humming, waiting for her return with the endless patience that had outlasted kingdoms and would outlast whatever came after.

The pattern was larger than any of them had imagined. But patterns, she was beginning to understand, could be rewoven by hands willing to hold the needle steady despite the pain of stitching truth into reality's torn fabric.

Whether those hands would be hers remained to be seen, but Amara felt she was ready to find out.

# CHAPTER 6
Caedric

The rabbit turned slowly over their small fire, its skin crackling as fat dripped into the flames with tiny hisses that punctuated the silence. Caedric tended the cooking, but his attention remained fixed on Amara as she sat warming herself by the flames, her sleeves pushed back to reveal the thread-like scars that coiled along her arms.

She'd been studying them for the better part of an hour, tracing their patterns with fingertips that trembled slightly in the firelight. Not from cold—the temperature was mild enough—but from whatever internal tension had been building since their escape from the ruins. Her scars pulsed with silver light to their own rhythm.

*She's changing,* he thought, watching how the light played across features that had grown sharper, more defined, as if proximity to the loom fragment had refined her essence in ways that transcended physical appearance. She's *becoming something the Guild has always warned about.*

The lessons echoed in his memory with uncomfortable clarity. Master Korren's voice during his second year of training, describing the fate that awaited those who let supernatural power consume their humanity.

*"The gift becomes the person, Unraveler. Thread by thread, voice by voice, until nothing remains but echoes wearing flesh. They cease to be individuals and become conduits for forces beyond mortal comprehension."*

Years of Hemlock Circle doctrine had drilled such warnings into his consciousness—stories of gifted weavers who'd lost themselves to the whispers in fabric, who'd unraveled their own minds thread by thread until their bodies moved like puppets guided by accumulations of the dead. Such practitioners had to be unmade before they tore reality's fabric further, their corruption dispersed before it could spread like an infection through the realm's carefully maintained order.

But doctrine felt inadequate when applied to the woman across the fire from him. She didn't move like someone losing her humanity—if anything, her responses had grown more nuanced, more deeply felt, as if the spirits in her blood had enhanced her rather than diminished. When she smiled, it carried warmth that no mere echo could replicate. When she spoke, her words held the weight of someone grappling with profound responsibility rather than surrendering to alien influence.

*Perhaps the Guild's warnings were wrong,* he thought, then immediately pushed the notion aside. *Or perhaps she's simply stronger than most who face such transformation.*

"I need to go back," Amara said suddenly, her voice faltering as if she knew she'd reached a decision knowing it wouldn't be well received. "To the ruins. The loom fragment showed me things, Caedric. Important things."

"It almost killed you. You collapsed, bleeding. That fragment wasn't offering gifts—it was trying to consume you."

"It was trying to show me the truth." She looked up from her scars, her eyes reflecting the firelight with unusual intensity. "The world is unraveling. It has been for centuries, so slowly most people never notice. But I can see it now. I can feel it in every thread."

"Seeing and surviving aren't the same thing." Caedric forced his voice to remain calm despite the fear clawing at his chest. "Whatever that thing showed you, it demanded a payment you can't afford to spend."

"And if I'm the only one who can repair what's been damaged? If my gift is the key to preventing complete collapse?" Her hands clenched into fists, scars flaring brighter with the gesture. "Then the payment becomes irrelevant."

The casual dismissal of her own life sent anger flashing through him. "No. Absolutely not. I won't let you throw yourself away chasing visions that might be lies designed to manipulate you."

"*Let* me?" The words emerged with dangerous quiet. "You won't let me? Since when do you decide what I'm allowed to do?"

*Since I chose you over everything else I've ever believed in,* he thought but couldn't say aloud. *Since your survival became more important than my oath, my honor, my entire understanding of right and wrong.*

"Since you started talking about sacrificing yourself for cosmic purposes you barely understand," he said instead. "Since you began treating your life like it belongs to forces greater than yourself."

"Maybe it does." She stood abruptly, pacing to the edge of the firelight. She was silent for a moment before she turned back around. "Maybe this was never about what I wanted or feared. Maybe some responsibilities transcend personal choice."

"And maybe that's exactly what those things want you to believe." Caedric set down the spit and faced her across the flames, his hand moving instinctively toward his thread-cutter's hilt. "Maybe surrender disguised as duty is still surrender."

The argument that followed was conducted in careful whispers—both of them too experienced to raise voices that might carry to listening ears. But volume had nothing to do with intensity, and soon they were facing each other like opposing forces, each convinced the other couldn't see crucial truths.

She thought he was treating her like a reckless child, incapable of understanding the scope of what she'd witnessed. He thought she was blind to manipulation by forces that viewed her as raw material for their own designs. Both accusations held enough truth to cut deep, but each saw only the shadow of the other's fear, not the love that cast it.

*She's afraid I'll try to stop her,* he realized during a pause in their heated exchange. *And I'm afraid she'll succeed in whatever self-destructive course she's planning.*

"I need air," he said finally, recognizing that continuing the argument would only drive them further apart. "Stay by the fire... please. I'll scout our perimeter."

He walked away before she could respond, following game trails that led deeper into the forest. The cool air helped clear his head, but it also revealed signs that made his blood run cold. Fresh horse tracks, too regular to be wild animals. Most damning of all, a scrap of fabric hanging from a thornbush—silk that had been deliberately severed with silver thread, its edges humming faintly with silenced echoes.

A Guild warning. The Hemlock Circle's traditional sign that they'd marked this territory for official business.

*They're not sending mercenaries this time,* Caedric thought, examining the cloth with growing dread. *They're sending Unravelers. My former brothers.*

Mercenaries could be outfought, outwitted, driven off with superior tactics and willpower. But Unravelers possessed training that matched his own, equipment designed specifically for supernatural combat, and most importantly, knowledge of his personal fighting style learned through years of shared instruction.

More than that, they would know him. Men he'd served beside, trained with, trusted with his life during dangerous missions. The thought of facing them in combat—of potentially killing people who'd been family in all but blood—made his stomach clench with anticipatory grief.

But the alternative was worse. If they took Amara alive, her fate would be determined by Pattern Council members who saw her as a resource to be exploited rather than a person deserving protection. If they took her dead, at least her suffering would end quickly.

*I won't let either happen,* he vowed, refolding the warning cloth and tucking it away as evidence of how close their pursuers had come. *Guild training or not, brotherhood or not, anyone who tries to claim her will find me standing in their way.*

When he returned to their camp, Amara was sitting by the fire again, but her posture had changed. Her shoulders had softened from their rigid line, her gaze fixed on something in the middle distance that only she could see, fingers absently tracing patterns in the dirt beside her.

"You're right," she said quietly. "About the loom fragment. It was dangerous, and I was too eager to find answers to properly assess the risks."

Her words should have eased his mind, but the cadence of her voice carried the unmistakable weight of someone who has merely paused to gather strength before continuing down a dangerous path.

"But I can't unknow what it showed me," she continued. "Can't ignore the responsibility that comes with understanding how fragile the patterns really are. If I'm truly connected to forces larger than myself, then I need guidance from someone who understands what that means."

"The Guild claims to understand."

"The Guild created the problem." Her voice carried absolute certainty. "They're the ones who cut the threads in the first place, who damaged the Loom through fear and desire for control. They can't fix what they broke because they still don't understand what they destroyed."

Caedric wanted to argue, but found himself remembering recent revelations about Guild corruption, their willingness to arm mercenaries with null-thread cloaks, their use of cultists as unofficial allies. Perhaps institutional wisdom had been compromised by the same forces that had driven them to hunt Amara with such desperate hunger.

"Then who can provide the guidance you need?"

"I don't know yet. But someone, somewhere, must understand what's happening to me. What I'm becoming." She looked up at him, the campfire revealing the exhaustion that lined her face despite her determination. "I just hope we find them before..."

She didn't finish the sentence, but Caedric heard the unspoken ending anyway. Before the voices in her blood overwhelmed whatever remained of her individual will. Before the transformation completed itself in ways that left nothing recognizably human behind.

*I must protect her not only from the Guild and cult, but from herself.*

The realization settled like lead in his chest. External enemies could be fought with conventional tactics, but how did one battle against forces that struck from within? How did he shield someone from their own nature when that nature might be the key to preventing cosmic collapse? If what she saw was true, anyway.

Later, as Amara drifted toward sleep beside their dying fire, Caedric took first watch with his thread-cutter across his knees. The forest around them had been quiet, but in the distance, barely audible even to his trained hearing, came the sound that made his breath catch in his throat.

Horns. Not the crude instruments farmers used to call livestock, but the precisely tuned brass that carried Guild signals across vast distances. Three long notes followed by two short ones—the call that announced a formal hunt was in progress, authorized by Pattern Council decree and carried out by Hemlock Circle enforcers.

*They're coming,* he thought, watching the stars overhead while calculating distances, travel times, tactical possibilities that all led to the same grim conclusion. *And this time, it won't be mercenaries. It will be my brothers.*

They would be skilled, determined, and absolutely convinced they served justice by claiming Amara for Guild purposes. In their minds, he was the traitor who'd chosen corruption over conscience, and she was the threat that required elimination before she could damage reality further.

The irony was bitter as medicine. He'd spent seven years hunting people like her, convinced that rogue weavers represented chaos that threatened the realm's stability. Now he understood that real chaos came from those who claimed authority over forces they'd never truly comprehended, who cut threads without understanding the patterns they destroyed.

But understanding wouldn't make the coming battle any less brutal. When his former brothers arrived—and they would arrive, as surely as dawn followed darkness— he would face the hardest choice of his life.

Stand with the Guild he'd served faithfully for seven years, or protect the woman who'd taught him the difference between following orders and serving justice.

The choice had already been made, really. Made the moment he'd cut down his colleagues in the Pattern Council chamber, made when he'd carried her from Guild territory despite direct orders to deliver her for evaluation.

But knowing the right choice and surviving its consequences were very different things. And as the horn calls faded into forest silence, Caedric began the grim process of preparing for war against everything he'd once held sacred.

# CHAPTER 7
## Amara

The forest grew wilder as they trekked closer to the mountains, and ancient oaks gave way to wind-twisted pines. Each step took them further from civilization and into territory where survival skills were crucial.

But distance brought no relief from the voices in Amara's blood. If anything, they grew stronger, more insistent, as if the proximity to wild places had awakened echoes that had slept for generations. The scars along her arms burned with constant fire, their silver light visible even through the fabric of her sleeves.

"The horns were closer at dawn," Caedric said, pausing to study tracks in the dirt. They might have been deer for all Amara knew. "They're gaining ground despite the rough terrain."

Amara nodded, but her attention was caught by something he couldn't perceive. Someone—or something—was observing them, but not with ordinary sight. Not the Guild hunters, whose presence felt like an approaching storm. This was different, patient.

*"She walks the old paths,"* whispered voices that might have come from the trees themselves. *"The one who listens without breaking, who binds without enslaving."*

The words made her stumble, one hand moving instinctively to the needle at her belt. But when she looked around, nothing moved except the wind through the heavy branches above.

"What is it?" Caedric asked, his thread-cutter appearing in his hand.

"Nothing. Just... the voices are restless."

His pale eyes studied her face with assessment, and she knew he was looking for signs of deterioration. She'd seen that look before, and it never failed to remind her how precarious her grip on sanity appeared to him.

They traveled for most of the day, making camp in a hollow between two boulders that offered protection from the wind and watching eyes. But even as Caedric built their small fire and prepared what meager food they carried, Amara felt the sensation of observation growing stronger.

Their appearance came without warning.

Three figures materialized from the shadows between the trees, moving in silence. They wore cloaks that seemed to capture and hold starlight, their faces hidden beneath deep hoods, their hands carrying lanterns that glowed with threads of woven fire.

Caedric's blade was out and ready before Amara could blink, his stance shifting into an offensive posture. The strangers made no aggressive moves, simply arranged themselves in a loose semicircle that blocked obvious escape routes.

"Peace, Unraveler," said the center figure, her voice soft. "We mean no harm to either of you."

"Guild rogues," Caedric said, his blade remaining unsheathed despite the conversational tone. "You should have been unmade years ago."

"Should we?" The woman pushed back her hood, revealing features that might have been middle-aged or might have been ageless—sharp cheekbones, silver-streaked hair, eyes that held depths like still water. "Or should the Guild have learned to listen before they chose to cut?"

Her companions followed suit, revealing faces bearing serenity. Not the twisted corruption Amara had seen in Wraithstitcher features, but something closer to the expressions worn by master craftsmen who'd spent lifetimes perfecting their skills.

"I am Serenya," the woman continued, her attention shifting from Caedric to Amara. "We are Memory Keepers, guardians of echoes the Guild would silence forever. And you, child, have begun to listen in ways that few can manage."

She recognized the words. *Threads remember,* Amara thought, hearing the phrase in Serenya's voice though the woman hadn't spoken it aloud. *And you have begun to listen.*

"Rogues and criminals," Caedric said, but his voice held less certainty than before. "The

Guild maintains order for good reason. Without control, without structure—"

"Without control, magic serves its practitioners rather than distant authorities," Serenya interrupted. "Without structure imposed from above, power finds its own natural patterns." Her gaze remained fixed on Amara. "The Guild fears what it cannot control. We preserve what they would destroy."

Amara felt the familiar tug of forces larger than herself, the sense that choices were being made for her rather than by her. But this time, the sensation didn't feel like manipulation. Instead, it was as if she stood at the center of currents she was finally beginning to understand.

"What do you want?" she asked.

"To offer sanctuary," Serenya replied. "To provide guidance you'll need if you're to survive what you're becoming. The Guild teaches control through suppression. We teach harmony through understanding."

Caedric stepped closer to Amara, his protective instincts clearly triggered by words that sounded too much like recruitment. "And in exchange?"

"Nothing. Knowledge freely shared, wisdom passed down through generations of practitioners who chose preservation over power." Serenya's smile held genuine warmth. "Though I suspect she has much to teach us as well."

The invitation hung in the forest air like incense, carrying promises of answers to questions Amara had been afraid to ask. But she could feel Caedric's tension, his conviction that these people represented exactly the kind of corruption the Guild existed to prevent.

*Who do I trust?* she wondered. *The man who's sacrificed everything to protect me, or the people who claim to understand what I'm becoming?*

"Show us," she said finally, earning a sharp look from Caedric that she chose to ignore. "If you truly offer sanctuary, prove it."

———◆———

The Memory Keepers' refuge lay hidden in a cavern system that opened like a flower carved from the stone, but where Amara had expected the rough functionality of a hideout, she found something that took her breath away.

Tapestries hung from every wall, their threads worked with silver sigils that pulsed with gentle light. But these weren't the twisted abominations she'd seen in the Wraithstitcher lair—each piece hummed with voices that carried warmth, comfort, and the love of lives fully lived.

The air itself felt alive with preserved memory, but not the chaotic chorus that usually overwhelmed her senses. Instead, the echoes had been woven together into harmonies that spoke of careful curation, of practitioners who understood how to preserve without corrupting.

"This is what the Guild destroys," Serenya said, leading them deeper into chambers that opened like rooms in a vast house. "Not just individual voices, but entire symphonies of human experience. Stories that should be remembered, wisdom that should be preserved."

Amara reached toward one of the tapestries without thinking, her fingers stopping just short of contact as she felt the depth of memory contained within its threads. Not just echoes of the dead, but fragments of lives that had been preserved with loving attention to detail.

"May I?" she asked.

"Of course. But gently—listening rather than awakening, feeling rather than forcing."

Something deep within her bones knew the difference mattered, even as her conscious mind struggled to articulate why. She touched the fabric with fingertips that barely made contact, opening her enhanced senses without trying to impose her will.

The voices that rose weren't the desperate whispers she'd grown accustomed to, but something richer, more complete. A mother's lullaby, sung to children who'd grown and had children of their own. A blacksmith's pride in work that had outlasted his hands. An old woman's quiet satisfaction as she watched her grandchildren play in gardens she'd helped plant.

The experience should have overwhelmed her, but instead it felt like coming home. These weren't fragments torn from unwilling souls, but gifts freely given, memories preserved by people who understood their value.

"How?" she whispered.

"Patience. Practice. Understanding that force breaks what gentleness preserves." Serenya's voice carried the satisfaction of a teacher whose student had grasped an important lesson. "The Guild teaches binding through dominance. We teach binding through partnership."

Beside them, Caedric stood with obvious discomfort, his hand never leaving his thread-cutter's hilt. "Unlicensed weaving is still unlicensed weaving. Good intentions don't change the law."

"Laws change," said one of Serenya's companions, a younger man whose cloak showed the intricate needlework that marked master-level skill. "Authority shifts. But memory endures, if someone cares enough to preserve it."

"You have a rare gift," Serenya continued, her attention returning to Amara. "The ability to bind without unmaking, to strengthen rather than breaking. Most practitioners must choose between preservation and power. You might be able to achieve both."

The words carried implications that made Amara's chest tighten. "What are you suggesting?"

"That hiding and running may not be your only options. With proper training, with understanding of what you truly are..." Serenya moved to another tapestry, this one showing patterns that seemed to shift and flow like living things. "You could weave a new order. Not the Guild's rigid control or the cultists' mindless destruction, but something that serves memory rather than authority."

*Leadership.* The word hung unspoken in the cavern air, carrying weight that made Amara's transformative scars pulse with responding light. The Memory Keepers weren't just offering sanctuary—they were offering purpose, a role that would make her something more than a fugitive or a victim.

But she could feel Caedric's disapproval like heat from a forge, his conviction that these people represented exactly the kind of corruption that led to societal collapse. He'd sacrificed everything to protect her from forces that would use her abilities for their own ends. Was she really considering alliance with another group that saw her as instrumental to their vision of change?

"I need time to think," she said finally.

"Of course. Rest here tonight, let the sanctuary's peace restore what flight has damaged." Serenya gestured toward chambers that opened off the main cavern. "Tomorrow, we can discuss what training might involve."

---

The sleeping alcove they provided was simple but comfortable—soft bedding, clean water, walls lined with tapestries that whispered lullabies in languages older than kingdoms. For the first time since escaping Deymar, Amara felt truly safe, protected not just by stone walls but by people who understood the weight she carried.

But safety brought its own complications. Lying in darkness while gentle voices murmured comfort from every surface, she found herself confronting questions she'd been too busy running to ask.

What did she want from life beyond mere survival? Was she content to remain hidden forever, using her gift only when desperation demanded it? Or was there something larger she was meant to become?

The loom fragment's visions haunted her memory—reality itself unraveling thread by thread, patterns that had held for millennia beginning to fail. If she truly possessed abilities that could address such cosmic damage, did she have the right to choose personal safety over universal responsibility?

*But whose vision of responsibility?* she wondered. *The Guild's? The Keepers'? The voices in my blood?*

Caedric lay in the next alcove, close enough that she could hear his breathing but far enough to provide privacy. He hadn't spoken against the Memory Keepers directly, but his body language had broadcast disapproval loud enough for anyone to read.

He saw them as another threat, another group that would claim ownership of her abilities for their own purposes. But what if he was wrong? What if the Keepers truly offered partnership rather than exploitation, understanding rather than control?

The question felt like standing at a crossroads where every path led into darkness, with only faith and instinct to guide her choice.

Around her, the sanctuary's tapestries hummed with preserved voices, their songs creating harmonies that spoke of lives well-lived and love freely given. Not the desperate cries of souls torn from unwilling flesh, but the willing gifts of people who understood that memory was a treasure worth preserving.

She realized she wasn't afraid of the whispers now, but she *was* afraid of how much she wanted to listen to them.

The thought followed her into dreams where ancient looms stretched across starlit skies, their frames holding patterns too vast for mortal minds to comprehend. But in the dreams, she wasn't running from such forces—she was learning to work alongside them, her needle moving with cosmic rhythms that transformed the chaos into meaning.

Amara slept more peacefully than she had in a long while.

# CHAPTER 8
## Caedric

The Memory Keepers' sanctuary felt like a trap disguised as a temple. Caedric stood in the main cavern's entrance, his thread-cutter within easy reach, studying tapestries that glowed with preserved voices while every instinct honed by years of Guild training screamed warnings.

The chamber was undeniably beautiful—silver-threaded hangings that caught and held the light, voices that rose and fell in harmonies too perfect to be accidental. But beauty had nothing to do with corruption. Some of the most dangerous rogues he'd encountered had been artists, practitioners who used aesthetic appeal to mask the violations they performed on unwilling souls.

*Different methods,* he thought, watching how the tapestries seemed to breathe with their own rhythm. *Same desecration.*

The Guild's teachings were clear about places like this. Sanctuaries where voices accumulated beyond natural limits, where the boundary between life and death grew thin enough for dangerous things to slip through. Such locations became focal points for instability, tears in reality's fabric that widened with every echo added to their collection.

But as he watched Amara move among the hangings with something approaching reverence, touching fabric that responded to her presence with increasing warmth, he wondered if Guild doctrine had truly prepared him for the complexity of what they faced.

"She's remarkable," Serenya said, approaching with a silent grace that marked her as more than a simple rogue weaver. "I've preserved echoes for thirty years, and I've never seen anyone with such natural sensitivity to stored memory."

Her tone carried the warmth of a master craftsman admiring promising apprentice work, but Caedric heard undertones that made his skin crawl. Not quite possession, not quite hunger, but something that spoke of plans forming around Amara's abilities.

"Sensitivity can become vulnerability," he replied carefully. "Too much exposure to preserved voices has driven practitioners mad."

"Has it? Or have they simply learned to hear truths that others prefer to ignore?" Serenya's smile held a challenge beneath its courteous surface. "The Guild teaches that such experiences represent corruption. We've found them to be enlightenment."

She moved to stand beside Amara, who was examining a tapestry that depicted scenes from some long-ago harvest festival. The preserved voices rose in response to her attention—not desperate whispers, but joyful celebration, the happiness of communities that had trusted their memories to careful hands.

"See how she responds?" Serenya's asked, the pride in her voice undeniable. "No fear, no revulsion. She understands instinctively that these echoes chose preservation, that their presence here represents love rather than violation."

*She's not teaching Amara,* Caedric realized with growing unease. *She's claiming her.*

Master weavers took apprentices, certainly, but the relationship he observed between Serenya and Amara was beyond simple instruction. The older woman spoke to her with the particular attention reserved for someone whose potential exceeded normal bounds, whose abilities might serve purposes beyond personal development.

"Your scars mark you as chosen," Serenya continued, her fingers hovering just above the silver lines that coiled along Amara's arms. "The spirits who bound themselves to your essence saw something everyone else missed— a potential that goes beyond preservation into active restoration."

Amara's eyes brightened. "Restoration of what?"

"The patterns that have been damaged. The connections that have been severed. The harmony that existed before authority decided some voices mattered more than others." Serenya gestured toward tapestries that pulsed with responding light. "You could heal what the Guild has broken, child. Not through force or dominance, but through understanding and partnership."

The words struck chords that resonated through the cavern like music made from hope and possibility. But to Caedric's trained hearing, they carried the particular cadence of recruitment rather than simple education.

*Another dangerous ideology,* he thought. *Prettier than the Guild's doctrine, more seductive than the cultists' hunger, but ideology nonetheless.*

"How exactly does your work differ from what rogues do?" he asked, stepping closer to the conversation. "Unlicensed weaving is still unlicensed weaving, regardless of justification."

Serenya turned toward him with the patient expression of someone addressing willful ignorance. "We do not unravel, Unraveler. We do not bind unwilling spirits to purposes they never chose. We remember." Her gesture encompassed the entire sanctuary. "Every echo preserved here represents defiance against a world that forgets too easily, that discards wisdom in favor of convenience."

"And who decides which memories deserve preservation? Who determines whether spirits consent to eternal service?" Caedric's voice carried a dangerous edge, though he kept his hands away from his weapon. "Power over the dead is still power, regardless of how benevolently it's exercised."

"The spirits choose," Amara said quietly, her attention still fixed on the harvest tapestry. "I can feel it—their willingness, their gratitude for being remembered. It's not like what the Wraithstitchers do."

"Because they tell you it's different?" Caedric's frustration leaked into his voice despite his efforts at control. "Because they use prettier words to describe the same violations?"

The accusation hung in the cavern air, drawing attention from other Memory Keepers who'd been maintaining careful distance. Caedric found himself studying their faces, noting expressions that ranged from curiosity to barely concealed hostility.

Not all of them looked at Amara with Serenya's warm approval. Some watched her with the particular wariness reserved for dangerous animals, their postures suggesting readiness for flight rather than fellowship. Others displayed the hungry calculation he'd learned to associate with practitioners who saw power as a means rather than an end.

*Even here, she's seen as a weapon rather than a person,* he realized. *They just dress their ambitions in more attractive language.*

One of the younger Keepers—a man whose scarred hands spoke of long practice—muttered something to his companion that made both of them glance nervously toward Amara. Though Caedric couldn't catch the full exchange, fragments carried clearly in the cavern's acoustics:

"—too powerful—"

"—if she falters—"

"—cult will claim her before we can—"

The Memory Keepers weren't just offering sanctuary—they were positioning themselves for what they saw as an inevitable conflict over Amara's abilities. Whether she succeeded in mastering her transformation or collapsed under its weight, they intended to be the ones who determined her fate.

———◆———

"We need to talk," Caedric said later, finding Amara in the sleeping alcove Serenya had provided. The chamber was comfortable but not private—voices from the main cavern carried clearly through openings designed more for ventilation than concealment.

"About the Keepers?" Amara sat on the bed, her expression guarded but not hostile. "I know you don't trust them."

"They aren't allies," he said, keeping his voice low enough to avoid easy eavesdropping. "They're waiting for you to break, and when you do, they'll decide what to do with the pieces."

"Not everyone sees me as a curse, Caedric." Her voice was strained, and he knew she was weary of having the same repeated argument he was also tired of. "Some of them see hope. You only ever see danger."

The accusation stung because it held truth he couldn't entirely deny. His training had conditioned him to identify threats first and assess opportunities later, to err on the side of caution rather than trust. But that conditioning had also kept them alive through situations that would have destroyed more optimistic people.

"I see patterns," he replied. "The Guild wants to control your abilities. The cultists want to harvest them. And now the Keepers seek to channel your gift into their own vision, never asking if it aligns with yours. Everyone claims to know what's best for you except you."

"And what do you want?"

*I want you safe. I want you human. I want you to choose your own path rather than let others choose for you.* But the words felt too revealing, too much like a confession of feelings he wasn't prepared to examine.

"I want you to have choices," he said instead. "Real choices, not the illusion of freedom while others pull your strings."

Amara was quiet for a long moment, her attention seemingly fixed on patterns traced in the chamber's stone walls. When she spoke again, her voice was gentle, as if what she said would upset him.

"You're afraid they'll succeed where you've failed."

"What do you mean?"

"Teaching me control. Helping me understand what I'm becoming. Showing me that my gift doesn't have to be a burden." She looked up at him, her eyes reflecting the chamber's dim light. "You've tried to protect me by keeping me away from anything that might trigger my abilities. They're offering to teach me how to use them safely."

Her words felt like a knife between his ribs, cutting through assumptions he hadn't realized he'd been making. Had his protection become another form of cage, limiting her growth rather than enabling it?

"Safe for whom?" he asked. "For you, or for the purposes they want to put you to?"

"Maybe both. Maybe that's what partnership means—finding ways for everyone to benefit rather than demanding that someone sacrifice everything for others' comfort."

The words carried conviction that made his arguments feel hollow by comparison. She wasn't being seduced by false promises— she was weighing paths he had no right to close.

*Because I don't understand what she's becoming,* he admitted silently. *Because my training prepared me to fight corruption, not guide transformation.*

"Promise me something," he said finally.

"What?"

"If you decide to trust them, if you choose to accept their training, keep part of yourself separate. The part that belongs to you alone, not to any cause or ideology or vision of what you could become." He met her gaze steadily. "Because once you give that away, you can never get it back."

She nodded, but he wasn't certain she understood what he was asking. The Memory Keepers offered answers to questions that had tormented her since her transformation began. Against that, his warnings about abstract dangers probably seemed paranoid at best.

———◆———

Sleep proved elusive. Caedric lay in his alcove with eyes closed but senses alert, tracking movement and conversation from the main cavern. The Memory Keepers maintained watch rotations like any military unit, but their discipline felt different from the Guild's precision—looser, more collaborative, but also more secretive.

Around midnight, he heard Serenya's voice carrying from the tapestry chamber, speaking in the low tones reserved for sensitive discussions. Though he couldn't make out specific words, the rhythm suggested planning rather than casual conversation.

Moving with the silence he'd perfected during reconnaissance missions, Caedric eased from his alcove and approached the main cavern's edge. Shadows provided concealment while leaving him close enough to observe whatever was transpiring.

Serenya stood among the glowing tapestries, but she wasn't simply admiring preserved memories. Her hands moved in patterns he recognized from advanced weaving techniques, threads of silver light flowing between her fingers as she worked changes in the sanctuary's fundamental structure.

*She's weaving something,* he realized. *Some plan or preparation that requires altering the echoes themselves.*

The implications made his blood run cold. If Serenya could manipulate the preserved voices, could shape their messages or intentions, then everything the Memory Keepers claimed about consent and partnership became meaningless. The spirits might be saying whatever she wanted them to say, believing whatever she wanted them to believe.

When she finally finished her work and retired to her own chambers, Caedric remained in the shadows, studying tapestries that now hummed with subtly different harmonies. Not corrupt exactly, but now they sang with subtle undertones—like a familiar melody transposed to serve a hidden composer's intent.

*If Serenya thinks she can take Amara from me,* he thought, his hand moving to his thread-cutter's familiar weight, *she'll soon learn I've cut down finer threads.*

The promise felt like drawing a line in stone, marking territory he would defend regardless of the cost. The Guild had trained him to serve abstract principles, but this was different—personal in ways that transcended duty or doctrine.

Amara deserved protection not just from external enemies, but from anyone who would claim ownership of her choices. Even if those people offered wisdom he couldn't provide, even if they promised solutions to problems he couldn't solve.

Some things mattered more than solutions. Some people were worth defending even when they couldn't see the danger they faced.

As the light of dawn began to filter through the cavern's openings, painting the tapestries in shades of gold, Caedric made his own plans. Not for conquest or control, but for vigilance.

Whatever the Memory Keepers intended for Amara, they would discover that her protection came with complications they hadn't anticipated. And if it came to choosing between their vision of the future and her right to determine her own fate, there would be no contest about where his loyalty lay.

The threads of whatever web Serenya was weaving would find themselves cut by silver steel wielded by someone who understood that some things were worth any price to preserve.

# CHAPTER 9
## Amara

Dawn filtered through the sanctuary, casting prismatic beams across the ancient tapestries with a luminescence that seemed to give voice to their silent threads. Amara sat beside one of the glowing hangings, letting its gentle voices wash over her consciousness while she tried to make sense of the conflicting emotions that had kept her awake through most of the night.

Hope and fear warred in her chest with equal intensity. The Memory Keepers offered something she'd never dared imagine—teachers who understood her transformation, guidance that could help her master abilities that felt increasingly dangerous with each passing day. But Caedric's warnings echoed in her memory, reminding her that every group they'd encountered had seen her as a tool.

"You're awake early," Serenya said, approaching quietly. "Sleep comes hard when the voices are restless."

It wasn't a question. The older woman's eyes held the understanding of someone who'd walked similar paths, who knew firsthand the weight of memory pressing against mortal consciousness.

"They're louder here," Amara replied. "Not threatening, just... present. Like background music that grows more noticeable the longer you listen."

"Because this place was built to preserve them. Every stone has been worked with threads that hold echoes, every chamber designed to create harmony from what might otherwise be chaos." Serenya settled beside her, close enough for conversation but far enough to avoid crowding. "Would you like to begin understanding how that harmony is achieved?"

The offer carried the promises of answers to questions Amara had been afraid to ask. Behind them, she could hear movement from the sleeping alcoves—Caedric stirring, probably already reaching for his thread-cutter from habit.

"I have to learn," she said, making the decision before doubt could undermine her resolve. "I can't keep stumbling in the dark, hoping instinct will guide me through situations that require actual knowledge."

Footsteps approached from behind, measured and purposeful. "Knowledge can be more dangerous than ignorance," Caedric said. "Especially when it comes from sources with their own agendas."

Amara felt familiar irritation flare in her chest. "Everything has an agenda. Even protecting me has an agenda. At least they're offering to teach me rather than simply telling me what I can't do."

"Because they want something from you. Because they see your abilities as instrumental to the vision they're pursuing." His pale eyes fixed on Serenya with obvious distrust. "Just like everyone else."

"This is *my* choice," Amara said, standing to face him directly. "*My* gift, *my* transformation, *my* decision about how to understand what I'm becoming." The words came out harder than she'd intended, carrying frustration that had been building since their argument the previous evening. "I won't let fear keep me powerless forever."

Something flickered across Caedric's expression—hurt, perhaps, or recognition that she was moving beyond his ability to protect through simple authority. But he stepped back without further argument, his professional mask sliding into place to conceal his emotions.

"Be careful," was all he said.

◆

Serenya led her deeper into the sanctuary than she'd previously explored. The air grew thick as they descended, not oppressive but heavy with the weight of voices waiting to be heard.

"This is the Chamber of Threads," Serenya said, pausing before an archway that glowed with silver sigils. "Where we preserve the most precious echoes—not just fragments, but entire lives rendered into cloth."

The chamber beyond took Amara's breath away. Hundreds of garments hung from the walls and ceiling, each one humming with its own frequency. A child's dress sparkled with laughter. An old man's coat carried the satisfaction of work well done. A woman's wedding gown that glowed with joy so pure it made Amara's chest ache with sympathy.

Together, they formed a chorus that spoke of human experience in all its complexity— not just the bright moments, but the sorrows, the fears, the quiet desperation that marked mortal existence. Yet somehow, even the pain felt transformed by preservation into something that was honored rather than exploited.

"These are not tools," Serenya said, her voice carrying reverence that bordered on worship. "They are lives. We do not unravel or bind—we listen. To remember is to honor."

Amara moved among the hanging garments like a pilgrim in a sacred space, feeling how each piece responded to her presence with increasing warmth. The voices they contained weren't crying out for release or rescue—they were sharing, offering fragments of themselves freely to someone who understood their value.

"How do you choose?" she asked. "Which memories to preserve, which lives to honor?"

"We don't choose. They choose us." Serenya smiled. "The dying sometimes sense what we do, what we offer. They come to us in their final days, seeking preservation for what they hold most dear. Others we encounter by chance, drawn by resonances we don't fully understand."

The older woman moved to a section of wall where simpler garments hung—not the elaborate pieces that spoke of wealth or status, but common clothing that had been worn by people whose names history would never record.

"Would you like to try listening?" Serenya asked. "Not awakening, not binding, just opening yourself to what these echoes choose to share?"

Amara nodded, though her hands trembled as Serenya selected a particular garment from the collection. It was a shawl, its fabric worn thin by years of use, stained with substances that spoke of a life lived in hardship but not despair.

"Listen longer than you think you can bear," Serenya instructed, placing the shawl in Amara's hands. "Pain passes, but understanding endures. Let her story become part of yours, but don't lose yourself in the process."

The moment the fabric touched her skin, whispers rose like music. At first, they were fragments—glimpses of warmth by a winter fire, the scent of bread baking, children's voices calling from another room. Pleasant echoes that spoke of contentment despite material poverty.

But as Amara opened herself more fully to what the shawl contained, deeper currents began to emerge. The woman who'd worn it had known loss—a husband taken by fever, children who'd grown and moved away, friends claimed by time's inexorable passage. Each grief had been wrapped in this fabric, absorbed into its fibers like tears into cloth.

*Margaret,* whispered a voice that felt like her own thoughts but carried different cadences. *My name is Margaret, and I lived long enough to see my grandchildren.*

The boundary between Amara's consciousness and the preserved echo began to blur. She could feel Margaret's arthritic hands, could taste the bitterness of herbs taken for pain, could experience the weariness that came from outliving most of those you'd loved.

But beneath the sorrow lay something else—satisfaction, gratitude for time granted, acceptance of mortality as natural rather than tragic. Margaret had died wrapped in this shawl, peaceful in the knowledge that her story would continue through her children and grandchildren who carried her lessons forward.

*Remember me,* the voice pleaded with gentle insistence. *Not the pain, but the love. Not the endings, but the connections.*

Amara felt tears streaming down her face, but she didn't pull away. The shawl burned in her hands as her scars flared with responding light, the silver threads beneath her skin pulsing in rhythm with Margaret's preserved heartbeat. For a terrifying moment, she couldn't tell where her own identity ended and the echo began.

*This is how it happened,* she realized with growing alarm. *This is how practitioners lose themselves—not through force or violation, but through connection so complete it erases the boundaries between self and other.*

With desperate effort, she pulled back from the brink, using techniques learned through painful experience to separate her consciousness from Margaret's essence. The shawl's whispers faded to gentle murmurs, though she could still feel the echo's gratitude for being heard, for being remembered with love rather than fear.

"Well done," Serenya said, her voice carrying the satisfaction of a teacher whose student had exceeded expectations. "Most practitioners can barely touch such deep preservation without losing themselves entirely. You not only listened—you honored her while remaining yourself."

Amara wiped tears from her cheeks with hands that shook from more than exhaustion. "I almost didn't remain myself. For a moment,

I thought I was her—felt her pain, her memories, her acceptance of death."

"That's the gift and the burden," Serenya replied. "You carry them within you in ways others cannot. That connection—that empathy—is what makes your abilities so remarkable. And so dangerous."

The words should have been comforting, but they felt like confirmation of fears Amara had been trying to suppress. Each time she used her gift, each echo she awakened or silenced, she risked losing pieces of herself to voices that had their own agendas and desires.

———◆———

"Every time you do this, you let them in deeper," Caedric said when she found him in the main cavern, his voice tight with frustration and worry. "How much of you will be left when they're finished?"

The question struck too close to her own fears, making her defensive in ways that logic couldn't justify. "At least I'm trying to understand! You'd rather I stay afraid so you can play the protector."

"I'd rather you stay alive. Stay human. Stay yourself instead of becoming some vessel for other voices." His eyes blazed with emotion she'd rarely seen him display. "Every session pushes you closer to a line you can't uncross."

"And staying ignorant keeps me weak!" Her words sliced through the air between them, a blade honed on the whetstone of unspoken tension. "You want to protect me from everything, including knowledge that might actually help me survive."

"I want to protect you from losing what makes you worth protecting." His voice dropped to barely above a whisper, but the words carried a weight that made her chest tighten. "If you become just another echo in their collection, what was the point of everything you've sacrificed?"

The argument carved a chasm between them, and she didn't know how to bridge it. Amara could see hurt in his expression, recognition that she was moving beyond his ability to shield through authority or superior knowledge. But she could also see fear—not just for her safety, but for the connection they'd built through shared danger and mutual dependence.

*He's afraid I'll choose them over him,* she realized. *Afraid I'll find what I need from teachers who understand my gift better than he ever could.*

"This isn't about choosing sides," she said finally. "It's about learning to live with what I've become instead of spending the rest of my life running from it."

"And if what you become isn't you anymore?"

She had no answer for that question, because it echoed doubts that had haunted her since awakening with voices in her blood. But fear couldn't be the only guide for her choices—eventually, she had to trust in something beyond the certainty of danger.

That night, alone in her alcove while the sanctuary hummed with voices, Amara traced the glowing scars that coiled along her arms. For the first time since her transformation began, she didn't see them as wounds.

Instead, they looked like threads—silver connections binding her to echoes that had chosen her as their vessel, spirits that trusted her with their most precious memories. Not parasites feeding on her essence, but partners in a working larger than any individual consciousness.

The Memory Keepers understood that partnership in ways Caedric couldn't. They saw her transformation not as corruption to be feared, but as evolution to be guided. Under their teaching, she might finally learn to master abilities that felt increasingly dangerous with each uncontrolled manifestation.

But mastery came with prices that weren't always apparent until payment was demanded. Margaret's echo had nearly consumed her identity, had almost succeeded in overwriting Amara's consciousness with patterns that felt more complete, more experienced, more worthy of continued existence.

*Maybe Caedric was right to fear,* she thought, watching silver light pulse beneath her skin like a second heartbeat. *But if fear was all I had, I'd never become more than prey.*

The choice between safety and growth, between protection and agency, couldn't be delayed indefinitely. Tomorrow would bring new lessons, new tests of her ability to listen without losing herself. And eventually, she would have to decide whether the knowledge she gained was worth the risks it demanded.

# CHAPTER 10
## Caedric

The forest surrounding the Memory Keepers' sanctuary held different sounds at dawn. Birds chirped, a breeze rustled the leaves, and something skittered among the brush. Caedric sat on a fallen log thirty yards from the cavern entrance, his thread-cutter across his knees, listening to echoes that carried from within the hidden chambers. Amara's voice, raised in what sounded like instruction or explanation. Serenya's responses, warm with approval that made his stomach clench. The gentle hum of voices welcoming someone who understood their nature.

*She's going to lose herself to them,* he thought, watching silver light flicker briefly through the cavern's concealed openings. *Piece by piece, session by session, until nothing remains but another echo in their collection.*

The possibility filled him with cold rage that had nothing to do with Guild doctrine or institutional loyalty. This was personal. He burned with fury, helpless as he watched a loved one surrender to forces that would consume everything that made her unique.

*If she loses herself completely,* he vowed silently, *I'll end it myself before the Guild ever lays a hand on what's left.*

The promise felt like blasphemy against everything he'd been taught about preserving life and protecting the innocent. But preserving echoes of the dead wasn't the same as protecting the living, and he would not let Amara become another voice trapped in the Memory Keepers' tapestries.

Movement at the forest's edge caught his attention. It wasn't the random rustling of wildlife, but something different. He scanned the trees and saw them. They emerged from the treeline in perfect unison, a formation he recognized from his own years of training. Their black cloaks swallowed the dawn's weak light. Silver thread-cutters that gleamed with deadly purpose, and they approached with the familiar stance of hunters closing on marked prey.

*Hemlock Circle.* His former brothers-in-arms, come to finish what the mercenaries had failed to accomplish.

The crossbow bolts came without warning, whistling through air thick with morning mist to strike the trees and stones around the cavern entrance. Guild fletching marked each shaft, their points designed to punch through supernatural defenses. But these weren't meant to kill—they were meant to announce presence, to declare formal engagement under rules both sides understood.

Caedric counted five Unravelers in full combat gear, elite Guild hunters. At their head walked a man whose stance and bearing were as familiar as his own reflection. Taron Grimstead, the man who had once shared his bread during starvation drills, who had carried him three miles with a broken ankle through the Blackmire swamps, who had wept beside him when they burned their civilian clothes in the Ritual of Severance. Now he approached with the cold precision that had earned him the nickname "The Severant."

*Of all the hunters they could have sent,* Caedric thought with bitter irony, *they chose the one who knows my techniques better than anyone.*

"Caedric." Taron's voice carried across the clearing. "You should have cut her down the day you saw her. The fact that you didn't proves you've forgotten your oath."

The accusation hit like a physical blow, not because it was false but because it came from someone whose judgment he'd once valued above his own. Taron had been his anchor during the dark moments that came with hunting dangerous rogues, his reminder that Guild service meant protecting the innocent rather than simply eliminating threats.

Now he stood with silver blade drawn, convinced that Caedric represented the very corruption they'd been trained to prevent.

"My oath was to protect the Loom," Caedric replied, rising from his position with his own weapon ready. "Not to leash innocents for the Council's greed."

"Innocents?" Taron laughed. "She awakened the dead in the Guild Hall itself. Turned royal spirits into weapons against lawful authority. If that's innocence, then corruption has redefined itself beyond recognition."

The philosophical debate felt surreal against the backdrop of imminent violence, but Caedric recognized it as a necessary prologue. They'd been brothers once—they owed each other honest words before steel settled the questions that conversation couldn't resolve.

"She freed souls that would have been enslaved. Used forbidden power to restore mercy where none existed." Caedric moved into the combat stance they'd practiced together for years, muscle memory older than conscious thought. "That's not corruption— that's exactly what our oath should have protected."

"Then you've truly fallen." Taron's thread-cutter moved in patterns that mirrored Caedric's own, both men drawing on identical training to prepare for battle that would test everything they'd learned. "Come, then, brother. Let the Loom judge which of us serves truth."

Steel met steel with the intimacy of old friends. Taron feigned left before striking right, exactly as he had during winter training. Caedric countered with the half-step retreat their master had drilled into them beneath autumn rains. Their bodies remembered what their hearts wished to forget, and in the space between attacks lay the ghost of brotherhood, dying with each calculated strike.

The silver edge of Caedric's thread-cutter sliced through the air, humming with enchantment as it sought woven magic to unravel. Taron countered with his own blade—forged in the same Guild fires, blessed with identical runes—moving with the fluid precision that had earned him top marks in every combat assessment they'd endured together.

Around them, other Unravelers clashed with Memory Keepers. Guild-forged blades flashed against makeshift weapons—kitchen knives bound with memory-thread, farming tools imbued with ancestral strength.

*This is what I've brought them,* Caedric realized as he parried a thrust aimed at his heart. *Violence that will destroy everything they've spent decades preserving.*

But self-recrimination was a luxury he couldn't afford while Taron relentlessly pressed his attack. Each parry and thrust carried the weight of a thousand fireside conversations turned to ash, of brotherhood calcified into judgment.

"You were the best of us," Taron snarled as their blades locked in a contest of pure strength. "The most dedicated, the most faithful to our principles. What did she offer that was worth throwing all of that away?"

*Choice,* Caedric thought but couldn't speak aloud. *The chance to protect someone rather than serve an institution. The opportunity to choose mercy over law when law demanded cruelty.*

Instead, he twisted away from the blade-lock and drove his elbow toward Taron's ribs, using techniques he'd learned for close-quarters combat. But his opponent anticipated the move, stepping aside with fluid grace before launching a counterattack that opened a line of fire across Caedric's shoulder.

The battle raged through the clearing as dawn strengthened around them, neither side gaining a decisive advantage. But as sweat stung his eyes and his muscles burned with exertion, Caedric recognized the fundamental divide between them. Taron fought to eliminate a specific target, while he fought to protect the entire sanctuary and everyone within it.

The distinction changed everything about his tactics and priorities.

When Amara emerged from the cavern, her hands already working thread and needle in patterns that called forth spectral defenders, Caedric saw opportunity where others might have seen complication. Her echoes couldn't touch the Unravelers directly—their gear included null-thread protection designed specifically for such encounters. But they could affect the environment in ways that created tactical advantages.

"The tapestries!" he called to her, parrying another of Taron's increasingly desperate attacks. "Bring down the hanging banners!"

Understanding flashed across her face. The sanctuary's entrance was lined with preserved textiles that hung from wooden supports—not just decoration, but structural elements that helped support the cavern's roof. If those supports failed, the resulting collapse would force the Unravelers to retreat or risk being buried under tons of stone.

Amara's needle flew through rapid stitches that awakened every echo in the hanging banners simultaneously. Dozens of voices rose in harmonized song, a coordinated effort by spirits who understood the threat their sanctuary faced.

Translucent fingers curled around the timber braces as phantom choruses hummed forgotten cradle songs, their eerie melodies vibrating through the rock until moisture beaded like tears on the cavern walls. The effect was subtle at first, then increasingly dramatic as ancient timbers began to crack under supernatural pressure.

Taron realized the danger and lunged toward Amara with killing intent, but Caedric intercepted the attack with a move that left them both locked in a deadly embrace. His thread-cutter's edge found the silver cord worked into Taron's left sleeve—not just decoration, but the oath-thread that had bound him to Guild service since initiation.

The cut was precise, surgical, severing institutional loyalty with the same skill they'd both used to eliminate supernatural threats. But instead of killing his former friend, Caedric had done something worse—rendered him oathless, exiled from the only purpose that had given his life meaning.

Taron screamed as the severed thread dissolved, its binding power released back into the cosmic forces had originally shaped it. The sound was not the cry of a wounded man but of a soul suddenly untethered from its purpose.

The remaining Unravelers realized their position had become untenable. The cavern's roof was beginning to sag as the support timbers failed, while spectral defenders made coordinated advance impossible. They retreated toward the forest, practically dragging Taron with them.

"You are no longer one of us, Caedric," called the squad's second-in-command. "When next we meet, you will die as a rogue."

The pronouncement echoed through the clearing like funeral bells, marking the end of a relationship that had defined his adult life. He was no longer a Guild Unraveler, no longer someone who served institutional authority over personal conscience.

He was simply himself, defined by choices he'd made rather than oaths he'd inherited.

The Memory Keepers who survived the assault stared at him with expressions that mixed awe with wariness. They'd watched him fight the Guild's hunters, had seen him sever his former friend's oath-thread with skill that spoke of intimate knowledge about how such bindings worked.

He was dangerous to them in ways they were only beginning to understand. Not an enemy exactly, but not quite an ally either—something new that didn't fit comfortable categories.

Amara approached with careful steps, her needle still gleaming with residual power from the working that had saved them all. Blood marked where her scars had flared during combat, but her eyes held gratitude that made his chest tighten.

"Are you hurt?" she asked.

"Just a flesh wound." The answer was technically true, though it didn't encompass the deeper injury that came from choosing exile over belonging. "The Guild will send others. This sanctuary isn't safe anymore."

"Because of you," Serenya said, her steps measured and cautious as she drew near, her body angled slightly away as if preparing to retreat at the first sign of aggression. "Because you brought Guild attention to our refuge."

"I chose to protect someone worth saving while the Guild saw only a threat to their monopoly." Caedric's voice carried steel that made several Memory Keepers step backward. "If that choice threatens your safety, I apologize. But I won't pretend to regret making it."

Serenya's gaze lingered on him, her eyes narrowing slightly at the corners—the same careful assessment she might give to a tapestry whose threads revealed contradictory memories.

"The Guild trained you well," she said finally. "Perhaps too well for their own comfort."

*They trained me to serve justice,* he thought. *They just forgot that justice sometimes requires defying those who claim authority over it.*

But such discussions would have to wait. The sound of distant horns suggested that Guild reinforcements were already mobilizing, probably alerted by communication crystals the Unravelers carried. The sanctuary that had seemed like a refuge was becoming a trap, and everyone within it would pay the price for harboring fugitives from the Guild.

———◆———

Alone after the immediate crisis had passed, while Memory Keepers debated evacuation plans and Amara tended to wounds suffered during the fighting, Caedric sat on his fallen log and contemplated the magnitude of what he'd lost.

Seven years of rising at dawn to train, of sharing meals with men who would die for him, of believing in something larger than himself—all cut away by his own blade. It was a choice that had seemed inevitable at the time but felt increasingly costly in retrospect. Now, staring at his hands, Caedric wondered what would come next.

*I thought I could walk between worlds*, he reflected, watching smoke rise from the damaged sanctuary. *Soldier and rebel. Protector and oathkeeper. No more. That path is gone.*

The Guild would hunt him now with the same relentless efficiency they brought to pursuing any rogue threat. His techniques, his habits, his psychological profile—all of it would be analyzed by people who knew him as well as he knew himself.

But strangely, the prospect didn't terrify him as much as it should have. For the first time since joining the Hemlock Circle, his obligations were simple, clear, uncomplicated by institutional politics or competing loyalties.

*The only oath I have left is the one I've chosen: to her.*

That vow steadied him now that all else had fallen away. The Guild, the brotherhood, the certainty of purpose—gone. Yet in their absence, he found something unexpected: the freedom to choose his own battles. If they must run, fight, or make their final stand against overwhelming odds, at least he would do so by his own judgment, not as another's weapon.

The freedom was terrifying. But it was also liberation from compromises that had slowly poisoned everything he'd once believed about duty and honor.

As the Memory Keepers prepared for an evacuation that would scatter their wisdom to wherever safety might be found, Caedric made his own preparations. Not for flight this time, but for the battle that would answer the question of whether one person's moral compass could outweigh the power that had stood for centuries.

The Guild would come for them again. But when they did, they would not face confused fugitives. They would find committed rebels.

# CHAPTER 11
## Amara

The blood had been cleaned from the sanctuary's stone floor, but Amara could still see where it had pooled—dark stains that marked the spots where Memory Keepers had fallen defending their refuge. Five dead, three wounded, and an ancient sanctuary compromised beyond repair. All because she'd brought Guild attention to people who'd lived in hidden peace for decades.

*He severed his past for me,* she thought, watching Caedric examine damaged tapestries. The emptiness in his eyes since cutting Taron's oath-thread worried her more than his physical wounds. *I can't keep faltering if I'm to be worth that sacrifice.*

The guilt sat heavily in her chest like a swallowed stone. Every person who'd suffered because of her presence, every connection

Caedric had severed to protect her, every moment of peace shattered by the forces that pursued her—all of it amassed into a debt she couldn't hope to repay.

She had to become something more than a fugitive, something more than a burden requiring constant protection. The question was whether she possessed the strength to transform without losing herself in the process.

"You're brooding," Serenya said. "Guilt serves no purpose beyond self-torture. What matters is what you do with the knowledge that people have died for your freedom."

The words should have been comforting, but they carried undertones that made Amara's senses prickle with unease. Not sympathy for her emotional state, but assessment of her value despite the complications her presence had created.

"I should have been stronger. Should have been able to defend this place without putting everyone at risk." Amara gestured toward the damaged chamber, where preserved voices whispered with increased urgency. "Instead, I nearly got everyone killed."

"Strength comes through testing, not through hiding." Serenya moved to stand beside one of the glowing tapestries, her fingers hovering just above the threads that pulsed with their own rhythm. "Listening is only the first step. If you want to survive what's coming, you must learn to weave echoes into tapestries of defense."

The suggestion made Amara's scars burn with the memory of her last attempt at a large-scale working. The Guild Hall, spirits bound to her essence, power that had nearly consumed her individual identity in service to forces larger than any mortal consciousness.

"My last tapestry nearly destroyed me," she said quietly. "The voices in the Guild Hall... I lost myself in them, became something that isn't entirely human."

"Because you fought against your nature instead of embracing it. Power hidden is power wasted. Power wielded with understanding becomes survival."

From across the chamber, Caedric's voice cut through their conversation. "Power wielded recklessly becomes suicide. She's not ready for workings of that magnitude."

Serenya turned toward him with the expression of someone whose authority had been challenged by inferior understanding. "Readiness is not a luxury she can afford. The Guild will send larger forces, better equipped and more ruthless than the squad you barely defeated. When they come, pretty words and protective instincts won't be enough to save anyone."

"And if the working kills her? If she loses herself to the voices and becomes just another echo in your collection?" Caedric's hand moved toward his thread-cutter, though he stopped short of drawing the weapon. "What purpose does that serve beyond satisfying your curiosity about her limits?"

The accusation hung in the air, revealing tensions that had been building since their arrival at the sanctuary. Amara found herself caught between competing visions of her future—Caedric's desire to protect her humanity at all costs, Serenya's willingness to risk everything for the chance at true mastery.

*Both of them see something in me,* she realized. *But neither sees what I see in myself.*

"I'll try," she said, the decision surprising even her. "Not because either of you thinks I should, but because I need to know what I'm capable of when I stop holding back."

———— ◆ ————

The training chamber had been hastily repaired after the Guild attack, its walls relined with new tapestries. But the space felt different now—not the serene sanctuary where she'd first learned to listen, but something closer to an arena where fundamental questions would be settled through trial and consequence.

Memory Keepers had gathered scraps from their damaged collection, fragments of garments that had belonged to villagers and travelers whose lives had been cut short by violence or disease. Each piece whispered with its own frequency, but together they created a chorus louder than anything Amara had attempted to work with before.

"Draw them together," Serenya instructed. "Not just awakening individual echoes, but binding them into unity. Let their voices become one voice, their memories become shared memory."

Amara threaded her needle with hands that trembled, her knuckles white with the effort of maintaining steadiness. The needle caught the light, its silver surface no longer merely metal but a conduit transformed by countless hours in her hands. Years of channeling her gift had changed its nature, leaving it suspended between the mundane world of tools and the realm where objects become vessels for something beyond understanding.

The first stitch drew blood that mixed with the thread, her scars flaring with light that painted the chamber walls in shifting patterns. One by one, she connected fabric fragments that had belonged to different people, different lives, different dreams cut short by mortality's inevitable claims.

Each voice rose as her needle connected it to the growing pattern, but instead of the chaotic chorus she'd expected, the echoes began to harmonize. The voices found each other like old friends across a crowded room, reaching past death's veil to touch memories they recognized in one another—the taste of first love, a child's laughter, the weight of grief—all the things that made them human despite the different paths they had walked.

The tapestry that emerged was unlike anything she'd created before. Not a defensive construct born from desperation, but a collaborative working that honored each contributor while serving a collective purpose. Light flowed through its threads, creating patterns that seemed to move with their own rhythm.

For a moment, she felt the intoxicating sense of connection that came from perfect synthesis—dozens of lives flowing through her consciousness without overwhelming her individual identity. She was herself but also more than herself, an individual thread in a weaving that encompassed experiences beyond any single mortal existence.

*This is what I could become,* she thought, watching light dance across the fabric. *Not just a vessel, but a conductor helping them find harmony.*

But the more threads she added to the pattern, the stronger the collective voice became. What had begun as a gentle harmony grew into something more demanding, more insistent, until individual whispers merged into a chorus that drowned out her own thoughts.

*Remember us all. Hold us all. Never let us fade.*

The voices weren't asking anymore—they were pulling at her consciousness with desperate hunger. Her vision filled with faces of the dead, each one requiring attention, each one insisting their story mattered more than the others.

*A mother who'd lost three children to fever.*

*A merchant whose caravan had been slaughtered by bandits.*

*A farmer whose crops had failed, leading to starvation for his entire family.*

Each tragedy demanded full attention, complete empathy, total remembrance. The weight of their suffering pressed against her consciousness like a physical force, threatening to crush what remained of her identity beneath their collective need.

Blood dripped from her nose as the scars along her arms burned like molten veins, power flowing through pathways that hadn't been designed to channel so much emotion. The tapestry writhed in her hands as if alive, its threads pulling tighter around her fingers until she couldn't tell where fabric ended and her flesh began.

*One more voice. Just one more. You can hold us all if you try.*

The seductive whisper promised completion, perfect understanding, the chance to become a repository for every memory that had ever been threatened by time's passage. All she had to do was surrender the last barriers between herself and the shared consciousness that wanted to claim her as their eternal vessel.

*So close,* she heard Serenya's voice as if from a great distance. *So close to becoming what she must be.*

But even as the voices pulled her toward dissolution, some deeper instinct screamed warnings about lines that couldn't be uncrossed. This wasn't growth or mastery—it was consumption disguised as transcendence, individual identity sacrificed to collective hunger that would never be satisfied.

Silver steel cut through the tapestry, severing connections that had taken hours to establish. The echoes screamed as their careful pattern dissolved, voices that had tasted unity crying out in anguish as they were separated back into individual fragments.

"No!" Serenya's voice cracked like breaking glass. "She was almost there! Almost ready to hold them all!"

But Caedric ignored her protests, his thread-cutter reducing the collaborative masterpiece to scattered scraps that whispered with fading voices. His arms closed around Amara as she collapsed, her body wracked with convulsions.

"If becoming means dying, she'll never be yours to shape," he snarled at Serenya, his voice full of fury.

———◆———

Recovery came slowly, measured in heartbeats that gradually returned to normal rhythm and vision that cleared enough to distinguish faces from shadows. Amara found herself in Caedric's arms, his presence an anchor against the disorientation that followed the sudden severing.

"I almost lost myself," she whispered, her voice barely audible even to her own ears. "For a moment, I wanted to keep them all inside me. To never let them go."

The words left her mouth like those of an addict confessing to craving something that had nearly destroyed her—a bitter truth about desiring what would ultimately consume her. The tapestry had offered everything she'd ever wanted—understanding, connection, purpose larger than individual existence. But the price would have been everything that made her uniquely herself.

*This is what the Memory Keepers want,* she realized with growing horror. *Not partnership or training, but transformation that erases individual identity in favor of collective consciousness.*

"Your gift calls to power," Caedric said quietly, his arms tightening around her trembling form. "But power doesn't care whether you survive the experience. It only cares whether you're strong enough to channel its forces to flow through you."

Around them, Memory Keepers gathered with expressions that ranged from disappointment to calculation. They'd witnessed something unprecedented—a practitioner who could bind dozens of echoes into collaborative working without losing control entirely. The fact that she'd survived the attempt made her more valuable, not less.

*They're not angry that I nearly died,* Amara thought, studying faces that showed professional interest rather than concern. *They're angry that I pulled back before completing whatever transformation they think I need to undergo.*

Serenya approached slowly. "You were so close, child. Close to becoming the threadbearer we've waited generations to find. With practice, with proper guidance, you could learn to hold them all without losing yourself."

"Could I?" Amara met the older woman's gaze steadily. "Or would I just learn to convince myself I was still human while they ate away whatever remained of my individual will?"

The question hung in the air, waiting to be answered. But Serenya's silence spoke louder than any words could have, revealing truths the Memory Keepers preferred to leave unexamined.

———◆———

That night, alone in her alcove, Amara traced the scars that coiled along her arms as she had several times before. They pulsed with their own rhythm, no longer simple wounds but something closer to veins through which otherworldly power flowed with each heartbeat.

The tapestry had shown her what she could become—not merely a vessel, but something approaching divinity, consciousness vast enough to hold every memory that had ever faced extinction. The temptation to reach for such perfection again pressed against her thoughts like physical hunger.

*This is how practitioners fall,* she understood with crystalline clarity. *Not through force or violation, but through offering them everything they've ever wanted at prices they don't realize they're paying.*

The echoes weren't leaving her blood, weren't fading into dormancy as they had after previous workings. They waited beneath her consciousness like wolves, ready to emerge the moment her defenses weakened enough to let them through.

The realization should have terrified her. Instead, it felt like understanding the rules of a game she'd been playing blind since her transformation began. Knowledge was power, even when that knowledge revealed how precarious her position truly was.

Time would bring new choices about what kind of person she wanted to become—someone who preserved her humanity at the cost of limiting her potential, or someone who embraced transcendence despite the price it demanded.

The gift would always call to power. But power, she was learning, could be chosen rather than simply accepted. And choice, however difficult, was the one thing that remained uniquely hers regardless of what forces sought to claim her essence for their own purposes.

# CHAPTER 12
## Caedric

The sanctuary's corridors felt too narrow for the rage building in Caedric's chest. He stalked through the hallways, his footsteps echoing off stone walls that had absorbed decades of whispered secrets. Behind him, Amara's exhausted breathing marked where she lay recovering from nearly losing herself.

*So close,* Serenya's words echoed in his memory like poison. *So close to becoming what she must be.*

His fingers clenched into fists as he recalled Serenya's tone—the way she'd spoken of Amara as if describing a half-finished tapestry rather than a woman fighting for her soul. It carried the same cold calculation he'd heard in Guild chambers, where master weavers debated which apprentices might yield the highest return on investment, their voices never acknowledging the lives being bartered. Different rhetoric, different justifications, but the same fundamental corruption that transformed individuals into instruments.

*The Guild, the cult, the Keepers—none of them see her,* he thought, his hand moving instinctively to his thread-cutter's familiar weight. *They only see what she can become.*

Something fundamental separated what a person could do from who they were. Potential was valuable, certainly, but it wasn't the same as the person who possessed it. Amara's abilities mattered less than her choice about how to use them, and her transformation meant nothing if it erased what made her worth protecting in the first place.

But the Memory Keepers spoke of her development as if individual consent was an obstacle to be overcome rather than a principle to be respected. They saw her reluctance to embrace complete transcendence as weakness rather than wisdom, her desire to preserve some part of herself as limitation rather than strength.

*Just like the Guild. Just like everyone else who wants to claim ownership of what she's becoming.*

The realization sent ice through his veins, confirming suspicions he'd been trying to suppress since their arrival at the sanctuary. The Memory Keepers weren't allies—they were another faction seeking to use Amara's abilities for purposes she hadn't chosen, another group that would sacrifice her humanity for the chance at significance.

He found Serenya in the main chamber, tending to tapestries damaged during the Guild attack.

"You're pushing her too hard," Caedric said without preamble. "Too far, too fast, without regard for what the strain is doing to her mind."

Serenya looked up from her work, her expression one of smug arrogance. "We are teaching her to survive forces that would destroy someone with less potential. Would you prefer she remain helpless when those forces inevitably manifest?"

"I'd prefer she remain human rather than becoming another voice in your collection."

Their conversation drew the attention of other Memory Keepers who'd been maintaining a careful distance. Caedric found himself the focus of hostile stares, marked as an outsider whose presence threatened their carefully maintained harmony.

"Human? Look at her scars, Unraveler. Listen to the voices that speak through her blood. She stopped being merely human the moment she bound those spirits to her essence. The only question now is whether she learns to control what she's becoming or lets it control her."

"Control through understanding, yes, not through surrender to collective consciousness that would erase her individual will." Caedric stepped closer, his voice carrying steel that made several Keepers reach for improvised weapons. "You're not teaching her mastery— you're preparing her for consumption."

"And you would keep her blind, a child with a needle she cannot safely wield." Serenya's voice sharpened with challenge. "Which of us is more dangerous to her survival? The teacher who shows her possibilities, or the protector who would limit her growth out of misplaced sentiment?"

Their philosophical clash revealed fundamental differences that couldn't be reconciled through argument or compromise. Serenya saw power as an end in itself, transcendence as a goal that justified any sacrifice. Caedric saw power as a means to preserve what mattered most—individual choice, human connection, the right to determine one's own fate.

"You want her for more than training," he said. "You want her for your cause. To set her against the Guild not for her own protection, but for your vision of how magical authority should be restructured."

Serenya met his accusation with silence, her lips curving upward in the unmistakable expression of a strategist whose hidden designs had finally been brought into the light. "The world is unraveling, Unraveler. Threads that held reality stable for millennia are fraying beyond repair. Would you rather she learn to sew them shut, or let everything fall into the cultists' hands?"

The ambiguous answer rattled him because it held a truth he couldn't entirely dismiss. The cosmic forces Amara had witnessed in her vision represented threats larger than anything he had seen before. If reality itself was collapsing thread by thread, perhaps individual autonomy was a luxury they couldn't afford.

But that logic led toward the same authoritarian certainty that had corrupted the Guild—the belief that some people were qualified to make decisions for others, that cosmic necessity superseded personal choice.

"Those are her decisions to make," he said finally. "Not yours. Not mine. Hers."

"And those decisions require understanding she doesn't possess yet. Understanding we can provide, if you stop interfering with her education." Serenya returned her attention to the damaged tapestry, dismissing him with casual authority. "Stand aside, Caedric. Let her become what she must become."

———◆———

The patrol route he established around the sanctuary's perimeter served multiple purposes—early warning against Guild or cultist approach, familiarization with the terrain that might become a battlefield, and space to think without Memory Keeper observation. But as evening settled over the forest, his circuit brought him close enough to overhear a conversation that made his blood run cold.

Two Keepers stood in the shadow between ancient trees, their voices low, but fragments carried clearly in the night air, revealing secrets they thought safely hidden.

"—letters sent to the Guild—"

"—Serenya's bargain will hold them off—"

"—long enough for the working to complete—"

Caedric moved closer through the underbrush. The Keepers' faces were hidden beneath deep hoods, their identities masked by darkness and distance.

"—she suspects nothing?"

"—trusts completely. The Unraveler is more suspicious, but manageable—"

"—when the time comes, he won't be able to stop—"

The conversation broke off as one of them noticed movement in nearby bushes—not Caedric's approach, but some nocturnal animal pursuing its own agenda. But he'd heard enough to confirm his fears.

*Someone among the Memory Keepers is feeding information to the Guild. Perhaps Serenya herself, or another Keeper using her as cover for their own betrayal.*

If the Guild knew their location, knew Amara's current condition, knew about her training with preserved voices—then every moment they remained here was borrowed time that would eventually come due with interest.

But more disturbing was the reference to "the working" and Caedric being "manageable" until some unspecified moment arrived. The Memory Keepers weren't just teaching Amara—they were preparing her for a specific purpose that required his neutralization when the crucial moment came.

It shouldn't have surprised him. He'd suspected the Memory Keepers' motivations from their first encounter. But hearing confirmation still felt like betrayal, another instance of people Amara trusted revealing priorities that superseded her wellbeing.

Caedric found Amara in her sleeping alcove, pale and weak from the day's failed tapestry but awake despite the late hour. Moonlight filtered through the crystalline formations, painting her features in silver and shadow, highlighting her thread-like scars.

"Couldn't sleep either?" she asked, her voice barely above a whisper.

"Too much to think about." He settled himself on the floor beside her bed. "How are you feeling?"

"Hollow. Like something was carved out of me when you cut the tapestry apart." She traced patterns in the chamber's stone walls, her movements restless despite obvious exhaustion. "But also relieved. For a moment, I wanted to keep all those voices inside me. I wanted the power, the belonging, the sense of being connected to something larger than myself."

Her words transported Caedric back to the hollow-eyed addicts he'd encountered during Guild service, practitioners who'd lost themselves to supernatural forces that promised enlightenment while delivering destruction.

"The gift calls to power," he said quietly, repeating his earlier words. "But power doesn't care whether you survive the experience intact."

"I know. Intellectually, I understand that what I felt was dangerous, probably fatal if pushed to its logical conclusion." Her eyes met his in the chamber's dim light. "But part of me wants to try again. Wants to see how far I can go before I lose myself completely."

*If she succumbs to that temptation, she won't need the Guild or cult to break her. She'll break herself.*

The thought filled him with fear beyond professional concern. This was personal—the terror of watching someone he cared about surrender everything that made them worth caring about was too much to bear.

"Don't," he said, his voice carrying more emotion than he'd intended. "Whatever the Memory Keepers promise, whatever they offer, it's not worth losing yourself. Nothing is worth that price."

"Even if losing myself means saving everyone else? What if the price of mending those unraveling threads is... everything I am?" Her questions held the weight of someone grappling with responsibilities too large for mortal comprehension. "The loom fragment showed me threads unraveling across reality itself. If my sacrifice could repair that damage..."

"Then someone else can make that sacrifice. Someone who chooses it freely, without coercion or manipulation." Caedric's hand moved toward hers before stopping just short of contact. "You didn't ask for this burden. You don't owe the universe your humanity just because you happen to possess abilities others want to use."

The words felt inadequate against the magnitude of what she faced, but they carried conviction born from watching too many good people destroy themselves in service to abstract principles. No grand design deserved to be built on the broken will of an unwilling architect, no matter how beautiful the pattern it promised to weave across eternity.

"What if choice is a luxury I can't afford?"

"Then we'll find another way. We'll keep looking until we discover a solution that doesn't require you to stop being yourself." He met her gaze steadily. "I promise you that much."

Later, alone in his own alcove, Caedric sharpened his thread-cutter. The silver blade gleamed with power designed to cut through manifestations, but tonight it felt like an anchor against the forces that threatened to sweep away everything he'd chosen to protect.

The Guild would come again—armed with better weapons, equipped with superior numbers, and more prepared than their first assault. The Memory Keepers would not cease their relentless guidance of Amara toward an enlightenment that threatened to erase who she truly was. And somewhere in the shadows, the Wraithstitchers waited for an opportunity to claim her abilities they'd harvest through torture and violence.

Against all of that, he had only his skill, his determination, and his absolute refusal to let anyone use Amara for purposes she hadn't freely chosen.

*If betrayal comes,* he vowed silently, testing the blade's edge against material that parted before its touch, *it will find my blade waiting.*

The promise felt like drawing a line in stone, marking territory he would defend regardless of odds or consequences. He'd already sacrificed his past for her protection—his future was equally expendable if that's what keeping her safe required.

Around him, the Memory Keepers' sanctuary hummed with voices that spoke of remembered love and wisdom, but beneath their gentle chorus, he heard darker harmonies—ambition disguised as education, manipulation dressed up as enlightenment, the same corruption that had destroyed his faith in the Guild.

The Guild, the cult, the Keepers—all of them wanted to claim Amara for their own purposes. But she belonged to herself, and anyone who forgot that would discover how expensive such mistakes could be.

His blade sang softly as he continued its maintenance, silver steel he would use to cut through any thread attempting to bind her to others' will. Whatever came next—battle, betrayal, or a final confrontation with forces too large to defeat—he would face it willingly.

The hunt was far from over, but the prey had acquired teeth, and anyone seeking to claim her would learn that some protections couldn't be overcome through superior numbers or ancient authority.

They would learn that love, properly armed, was sharper than any blade.

# CHAPTER 13
## Amara

Consciousness returned with an exhaustion that went deeper than physical fatigue. Amara lay still, her entire body feeling hollow. Beneath the weakness, her scars pulsed with faint silver light, reminding her of the chorus of voices she'd nearly bound into permanent harmony.

The memory should have terrified her—the moment when her consciousness had almost dissolved into a collective existence, when the boundary between her and the echoes had grown thin enough to step across. Instead, she found herself thinking about the power she'd briefly held, the intoxicating sense of connection that came from being the conduit for experiences larger than any single life.

*I touched something magnificent,* she thought. *For just a heartbeat, I understood what it meant to hold entire histories in conscious awareness.*

The shame came afterward, as well as the recognition that she'd nearly lost herself to forces she couldn't control, that only Caedric's intervention had prevented complete dissolution. But underneath the shame lay something more disturbing: disappointment that the experience had ended before she could explore its full implications.

*This is how addiction begins,* she realized. *Not with a single moment of surrender, but with an attempt to make ordinary existence feel inadequate by comparison.*

Footsteps in the corridor announced an approaching presence, but Amara didn't need to look to know who was coming. Serenya's particular rhythm had become as familiar as her own heartbeat during their time in the sanctuary.

"You're awake," the older woman said, entering with arms full of supplies. "I brought herbs for the pain, and water to restore what the working drew from your essence."

She moved around the chamber with grace, preparing tisanes that smelled of comfort and healing. But her attention remained fixed on Amara with an intensity that suggested her interest was about more than just her wellbeing.

"How do you feel?" Serenya asked, offering a cup that steamed with aromatic vapors.

"Hollow. Empty. Like something was taken from me when the connection broke." Amara accepted the drink gratefully, its warmth spreading through her chest that had felt cold since awakening. "But also..."

"Also what?"

"Also like I caught a glimpse of something I was meant to see. Something that's been waiting for me to become strong enough to understand it." The admission felt like a confession, revealing the depths of an ambition she'd been afraid to acknowledge even to herself.

Serenya smiled. "You touched greatness, Amara. You felt what it means to hold memory, to command it rather than simply being commanded by it. Do not mistake fear for failure."

Her assessment reframed what had happened. It wasn't a perilous error but a crucial lesson. Serenya settled herself on the edge of the bed, her weight creating a gentle depression in the mattress.

"Caedric sees only the danger," she continued, her voice carrying gentle reproach. "He would have you live small, hidden, using your gift only in desperate moments when survival demands it. But power that serves only preservation serves no one."

"And what would you have me do instead?" Amara asked, though something in her chest already knew the answer.

"Become what you are meant to become. Not a weapon in someone else's hands, not a victim fleeing, but a leader who shapes those forces according to her own vision." Serenya's eyes glittered with fanatic intensity. "The realm needs guidance from someone who understands what the Guild has broken, who can offer an alternative to their rigid control."

The mantle of leadership meant facing what she'd been running from since her gift's first stirrings. Yet within that burden glimmered a possibility too precious to name:

she could walk in daylight as Amara, not merely as prey scurrying from the Guild's hunters.

"I don't know how to lead," she said quietly. "I barely know how to control my own abilities."

"Control comes through practice. Leadership comes through experience." Serenya rose and moved to one of the chamber's tapestries, her fingers hovering just above threads that glowed with memory. "Would you like to see what one of my predecessors accomplished? What's possible when power serves a purpose larger than survival?"

Without waiting for answer, she activated whatever working had been woven into the fabric's patterns. Light flowed through silver threads as voices rose in harmonized song—not the chaotic chorus that had nearly consumed Amara, but a symphony of the willing dead, each voice offering to be part of something greater than themselves.

The vision that emerged was breathtaking in its scope and beauty. A small village caught between warring kingdoms, its people mere pawns to greater powers. Yet around them gleamed a translucent dome—not of stone or steel, but woven from memories of love and loss. For three days this barrier held firm against armies that would have trampled the innocent, buying precious time for evacuation. At its center stood a single weaver, channeling not her own power but the collective strength of those who had chosen to stand together rather than kneel separately.

"Maeva was her name," Serenya said softly. "She died maintaining that working, but seven hundred people lived because she chose to spend her life preserving theirs. The Guild called her a rogue, the local nobility branded her a criminal, but history remembers her as hero."

The implication was clear without being stated directly. Amara could achieve similar greatness if she chose to embrace her potential rather than hiding from it, could become protector for those who had no other shield against the forces that would consume them.

"The people already whisper your name," Serenya continued, deactivating the vision with a gesture that returned the tapestry to a normal appearance. "Stories of the thread-witch who defied the Guild has spread from village to village, growing in scope and significance with each telling. Why not give them a banner to follow? Why not become a symbol of resistance against authority that serves only itself?"

The questions struck chords that resonated through every doubt and fear Amara had carried since her transformation began. She'd spent so long defining herself by what she was running from that she'd never considered what she might be running toward—creating something worth living for, something that might outlast her own existence.

*But at what cost?* she wondered, remembering the moment when collective consciousness had nearly claimed her entirely. *How much of myself would I have to sacrifice to become what others need me to be?*

"I need time to think," she said finally.

"Of course. Such decisions shouldn't be made hastily." Serenya moved toward the chamber's exit, then paused with her hand on the doorframe. "But remember—while you're thinking, others are suffering. The Guild tightens its grip on magical practice, the cultists harvest souls with increasing boldness, and common folk die because no one with power chooses to protect them."

Her challenge hung in the air long after the door closed behind her. How could Amara justify hiding when her abilities could shield those who had no other protection? How could she choose safety while others paid for her silence with their blood?

———◆———

"What did she want?"

Caedric's voice cut through her brooding, sharp with suspicion that had become his default response to any Memory Keeper interaction. He stood in the chamber's entrance, his pale eyes scanning for threats that might be present but invisible.

"To check on my recovery. To offer guidance about what comes next." Amara met his gaze steadily, though she didn't mention the specific nature of Serenya's suggestions. "The same things any teacher would do for a student who'd nearly been consumed by their own abilities."

"She's not your teacher. She's a collector who sees your power as another treasure to display in her gallery of useful artifacts." He moved into the chamber, his attention divided between her face and the tapestry Serenya had activated. "What did she show you?"

"Nothing dangerous. Just a glimpse of someone who used their gift to shield the innocent instead of ruling over them."

"And she positioned herself as a guide who could help you achieve similar greatness?" Caedric's voice carried bitter understanding. "Let me guess—the Guild represents rigid authority, the cultists embody mindless destruction, but the Memory Keepers offer a third path that honors your true potential."

The accuracy of his assessment stung because it revealed how transparent Serenya's manipulation had been. But it also suggested that he viewed her potential for anything beyond staying alive as dangerous territory, a precipice rather than a path.

"What if she's right?" Amara asked, surprising herself with the question's directness. "What if hiding and running aren't my only options? What if I could become something more than a victim fleeing from forces I can't control?"

"Then you'd become a target for every faction that wants to claim your abilities for their own purposes." Caedric's voice hardened with conviction. "The moment you step into open leadership, you stop being a person and become a symbol. And symbols belong to whoever can control their meaning."

"At least she doesn't treat me like a weapon about to explode. At least she believes I'm capable of growth rather than simply containing damage." The words emerged with heat that surprised them both, revealing frustrations she'd been suppressing since their argument about the loom fragment.

"I believe you're capable of choice. The choice to remain yourself rather than becoming what others need you to represent." His eyes bored into hers. "But that choice requires understanding what you'd be giving up, not just what you might gain."

The argument that followed was conducted in careful whispers—both of them too experienced to risk being overheard by Memory Keepers who might use their conflict for their own purposes. But volume had nothing to do with intensity, and soon they were facing each other across an emotional chasm that seemed to widen with each exchange.

He thought she was being seduced by false promises of significance that would ultimately destroy her humanity. She thought he was trapped in protective instincts that would keep her weak and dependent forever. Both accusations held enough truth to cut deep, while missing the deeper currents that drove their conflict.

*He's afraid of losing me to forces he can't fight, and I'm afraid of remaining small when I could become something more.*

But understanding the nature of their disagreement didn't resolve it. If anything, the clarity between them only deepened the divide, turning what might have been a bridge of understanding into a chasm neither knew how to cross.

When Caedric finally left—stalking away with his jaw clenched and his hand moving toward his thread-cutter—Amara found herself alone with questions that felt larger than her ability to answer them.

Voices spoke to Amara of responsibility and power and choices. Among them, Sarah's childish laughter, Captain Thorne's steady courage, the royal spirits who'd supported her defiance in the Guild Hall. New threads began to emerge. Not individual consciousness, but a collective harmony that spoke with a single voice despite being composed of dozens of distinct echoes.

*Threadbearer,* they whispered in unison. *Leader. Fate. The pattern calls to you.*

*You have touched the great weaving and felt its pull. You have heard our chorus and know its power. Why do you hesitate to claim what was always yours?*

Their words suggested a destiny that had been waiting for her to become strong enough to accept it. But beneath their harmonious surface lurked a familiar ravenous intent— the same devouring presence she had felt when the collective consciousness had nearly swallowed her selfhood whole.

Were these truly her own thoughts, or something else speaking through pathways the failed tapestry had carved in her mind?

*I told myself I didn't believe Serenya, but the threads did—and they were waiting for me to answer.*

It felt like she was beginning to understand a fundamental truth about her nature that she'd been avoiding. The voices in her blood weren't just passengers or partners—they were a chorus seeking a conductor, memories desperate for a weaver who could bind their disparate threads into a tapestry with meaning.

Whether she was strong enough to provide that guidance without losing herself in the process remained the central question of her life. Caedric said the gift would always call to power. But power, she was beginning to understand, could be shaped by will as much as will could be shaped by power.

The question was whether she possessed the strength to maintain that balance, or whether the forces gathering around her would tip the scales toward transformation she couldn't survive intact.

# CHAPTER 14
## Caedric

Tension stretched across the sanctuary like a bowstring drawn too tight—every footfall muffled, every conversation hushed, every face a mask of forced composure while hands lingered near weapons that shouldn't be needed in a place of refuge. Caedric had seen such atmospheres during his Guild years, the eerie stillness that descended when men knew blood would be shed but not whose or when the first arrow would fly.

*Everyone's waiting for a knife to fall,* he thought, completing another circuit of the hidden cavern's perimeter. *The only question is who's holding it.*

Memory Keepers went about their routines with forced normalcy, tending tapestries and maintaining the preserved voices that gave their sanctuary meaning. But their routines betrayed a hidden disquiet—glances that lingered too long on exits, conversations that died when he approached, the alertness that marked people keeping secrets from someone they considered dangerous.

Even Amara seemed different since her conversation with Serenya. More thoughtful, more distant, as if part of her attention had been captured by possibilities she couldn't quite articulate. When she looked at him, he caught glimpses of evaluation in her gold-flecked eyes—not suspicion exactly, but assessment of where his loyalties would fall if forced to choose between her safety and her ambitions.

*She's being turned against me,* he realized with cold certainty. *Slowly, carefully, with words that make my protection seem like a limitation rather than love.*

The realization should have prompted immediate action—confrontation with Serenya, demand for an explanation, perhaps even preparations for a tactical withdrawal if the sanctuary had been compromised. But the growing awareness that any move he made might push Amara further toward those who whispered of greatness rather than safety kept him from doing anything.

A sound from the deeper chambers drew his attention—not the gentle hum of echoes, but something sharper, more urgent. Footsteps in corridors that should have been empty, voices speaking in tones meant to avoid casual observation.

Caedric moved through shadows, his enhanced hearing picking up fragments of conversation.

"—the girl is ready—"

"—Guild will know when to strike—"

"—she suspects nothing—"

Through a gap in partially closed curtains, he saw figures that confirmed his worst suspicions. Serenya stood in conference with someone whose cloak bore Guild colors, their hands punctuating hushed words with sharp, precise gestures.

The messenger—for that's clearly what the Guild representative was—waved toward the main chamber where Amara rested between training sessions. "The Pattern

Council grows impatient. How much longer before she's ready for extraction?"

"Soon," Serenya replied, her voice carrying none of the warmth she'd shown when speaking with Amara. "Another day or two of preparation, and she'll be sufficiently destabilized to accept Guild custody as rescue rather than capture."

"And the Unraveler?"

"Will be dealt with when the time comes. His attachment to her makes him predictable, manageable until he's no longer useful." Her smile held a coldness that infuriated him. "By the time she realizes what's happening, it will be too late for either of them to resist."

Fury coiled in his gut like molten steel. He'd suspected the Memory Keepers' motivations from their first encounter, had sensed the manipulation beneath their offers of guidance and sanctuary. But hearing the confirmation still felt like betrayal.

*This was never about teaching her control. It was about breaking down her defenses so the Guild could claim her without resistance.*

His hand moved toward his weapon, muscles tensing for the strike that would end

Serenya's treachery before it could reach fruition. But uncertainty stayed the killing blow. If he acted too soon, Amara might never believe his warnings about the Memory Keepers' true nature. If he waited, she might be betrayed before he could prevent it.

He began to realize there may be no clean solution.

Caedric watched as the Guild messenger slipped away through a hidden fissure in the rock wall—another secret this sanctuary had kept from him. Serenya remained behind, adjusting tapestries with movements that seemed casual but carried the tension of someone preparing for action.

*How long do we have?* he wondered. *Hours? Days? And what happens when—*

The sanctuary shook with a sound like thunder, the reverberations sending dust cascading from the ceiling while preserved voices rose in alarm throughout the chamber. Not the measured assault of Guild forces, but something wilder, more chaotic.

*Wraithstitchers.*

Screams erupted from the main cavern, but these weren't human cries— they were the wails of the dead yanked back from peace and forced into servitude, echoes that had been twisted into weapons by barbed needles wielded with surgical malice.

Caedric ran toward the sounds of battle, drawing his thread-cutter. Behind him, he heard Serenya cursing, the architecture of her schemes collapsing around her like a tapestry suddenly cut from its frame.

The main chamber had been transformed into a vision from nightmare. Figures in stained robes moved through smoke and shadow, their barbed instruments weaving patterns that made reality bend around their points. At their head strode someone who radiated authority like furnace heat— gaunt and towering, wrapped in fabric that devoured every stray beam of light that dared touch its surface.

The Weaver of Bone. Caedric had heard descriptions during Guild briefings, but witnessing the man's presence firsthand was like staring into an abyss that stared back.

Memory Keepers fought with desperate courage, their tapestries coming alive as spectral defenders materialized to protect the sanctuary they'd spent decades building. But the Wraithstitchers countered with abominations that turned preserved love into weapons of hate, gentle echoes into screaming horrors that clawed at anyone within reach.

Through the chaos, Caedric caught glimpses of Amara pressed against the chamber's far wall, her scars blazing with silver fire as instinct overrode conscious thought. Her needle moved in patterns too fast to follow, weaving defenses from scraps of fabric while voices in her blood rose to meet the supernatural cacophony that filled the air.

*She's holding her own,* he realized with a mixture of pride and terror. *But for how long?*

A Wraithstitcher lunged at him with a needle aimed at his throat, but Caedric's blade was already moving, silver steel cutting through corrupted flesh to find the man's heart. Blood sprayed across the stone wall as he collapsed.

But there were too many of them, and more kept coming. The sanctuary's defenses—physical and supernatural—were being overwhelmed by enemies who fought with coordination born from decades of practice.

*This isn't a random attack,* he understood with growing alarm. *They knew exactly where to strike, exactly when we'd be most vulnerable.*

Movement at the chamber's edge confirmed his suspicions. Guild soldiers in full combat gear emerged from a hidden tunnel, revealing their attack had been orchestrated alongside the Wraithstitchers' onslaught. Leading them was the same messenger who'd been conferring with Serenya, his presence revealing the terrible truth. This was no coincidence, but a coordinated strike.

*This was a trap. And we were always the bait.*

The Memory Keepers hadn't been planning to betray Amara to the Guild—they'd been coordinating with multiple factions, playing all sides against each other while positioning themselves as final arbiters of her fate.

But their careful schemes were collapsing into chaos as Guild and cult found themselves in direct confrontation, each convinced they had exclusive claim to the prize they'd been promised.

A spectral defender materialized beside him—not one of the Memory Keepers' preserved echoes, but something that glowed with a silver light he recognized. One of the spirits bound to Amara's blood, manifesting to protect her through protective instinct rather than command.

*She's losing control,* he thought, watching how the spirit's form wavered between coherence and dissolution. *The stress is making her gift react without conscious direction.*

He carved through the melee with ruthless efficiency, his thread-cutter severing supernatural manifestations and mundane materials alike. Each strike brought him closer to Amara, who stood like a silver beacon amid the storm of enemies converging around her.

Every step toward her exacted its toll in blood and pain, his body collecting injuries faster than his mind could ignore them. A barbed needle scraped across his ribs, leaving a line of fire that promised infection if he survived long enough for healing to matter. A Guild soldier's blade found the gap in his defense, opening a cut along his sword arm that weakened his grip without completely disabling it.

*Too many enemies. Too little time. If we don't break free soon, we'll be overwhelmed.*

The Weaver of Bone turned toward him, his attention like ice sliding down Caedric's spine. When he spoke, his voice emerged with the whispers of countless souls woven into each syllable, their agony pulled taut across the warp and weft of his words.

"The threadbearer is ours, Unraveler. Stand aside and die quickly. Interfere, and learn what eternity means to those who oppose the Great Unraveling."

"She belongs to herself," Caedric replied, though his voice felt small against the supernatural cacophony that surrounded them. "And anyone who forgets that will learn how expensive such mistakes can be."

The man's laugh was a sound like breaking glass mixed with dying screams. "Brave words from someone whose blade cannot touch what I have become. Watch as I claim her essence thread by thread, until nothing remains but a voice in my collection."

*If Amara falls here, if the cult claims her abilities or the Guild seizes her, the world will unravel with her,* Caedric thought, raising his thread-cutter against an enemy who emanated malevolence beyond mortal measure.

Around them, the battle reached a crescendo of violence that threatened to bring down the sanctuary's ancient walls. Memory Keepers fell beside their tapestries, Guild soldiers discovered that Wraithstitcher needles drew no distinction between ally and enemy, and through it all, Amara's light continued to grow brighter.

# CHAPTER 15
## Amara

The darkness had weight, pressing against her consciousness like fabric. Amara struggled toward awareness through layers of confusion that seemed to multiply with each attempt to grasp coherent thought. When consciousness finally came, she found herself bound not by rope or chain, but by threads that pulsed with their own malevolent life.

The stitches woven against her skin glowed with sickly light, each thread carved from memory she recognized but couldn't quite place. Her grandmother's hands teaching her to sew. The first echo she'd ever awakened. The moment in the Guild Hall when spirits had bound themselves to her blood. All of it twisted into restraints that turned her own history into a prison.

She tried to call upon her gift, to awaken some scrap of fabric that might carry friendly voices, but the memory-threads burned like molten wire whenever she reached toward her abilities, pain so intense it left her gasping and blind.

*Stitched into silence,* she realized with growing horror. *They've bound my gift with my own memories, made my power turn against itself.*

The technique was sophisticated beyond anything she'd encountered—not just suppression, but corruption that used her deepest connections to render her abilities inaccessible. Whoever had woven these restraints understood her gift better than she understood it herself.

Footsteps echoed in the darkness, accompanied by voices that whispered in languages she didn't recognize. Hands seized her arms and lifted her from the surface she'd been lying on.

The chamber they brought her to defied every assumption she'd held about underground spaces. Instead of a rough cavern or utilitarian dungeon, she found herself in something that might have been a cathedral if cathedrals were built to honor forces that fed on suffering.

Vaulted ceilings disappeared into shadows that seemed to move with their own purpose, while walls rose in graceful arches that would have been beautiful if they hadn't been constructed from materials that made her stomach lurch. Bone formed the structural elements—not a random accumulation, but careful arrangement that spoke of architectural planning guided by aesthetic principles she couldn't begin to fathom.

Between the bones, stretched like parchment, hung scrolls of human skin that glowed with phosphorescent text. Not words exactly, but patterns, symbols that seemed to shift when observed peripherally.

*The Bone Cloister,* whispered voices that might have come from the walls themselves. *Where echoes never fade, never rest, never find peace.*

The air hummed with a presence that dwarfed anything she'd experienced in the Memory Keepers' sanctuary. But where their preserved voices had spoken of love and loss and lives fully lived, these echoes carried only hunger—endless, consuming need that pressed against her mind like fingers seeking purchase in her mind.

They wanted something from her. Not just her abilities, not just her compliance, but some key part of her nature that they believed could satisfy whatever void existed at their center.

Movement at the chamber's far end drew her attention toward a figure that seemed like something out of a nightmare. Tall, thin, and wearing robes that seemed to snuff out the light, the approaching presence made every memory-thread binding her flare with responding energy.

When he spoke, his voice carried layers—young and old, male and female, human and inhuman—a patchwork of echoes bound into a single throat that should never have been able to contain such complexity.

"Welcome, threadbearer," said the Weaver of Bone. "We have waited so long to meet you."

Up close, his presence was nauseating yet magnetic in ways that defied rational explanation. The mask he wore had been carved from a single piece of bone, its surface worked with sigils that pulsed with energy. It was his voice that truly disturbed her. Not the supernatural layers, but the underlying gentleness.

"You are afraid," he observed, settling into a chair in front of her. "They have told you we are monsters, creatures who delight in suffering for its own sake. But that is propaganda, child. We are keepers of memory too, only we are honest about its hunger."

His certainty slithered beneath her defenses, finding purchase in the cracks of her conviction—the same fractures that had been spreading since her transformation began. How different was her gift from what the Wraithstitchers practiced? Both involved binding spirits to physical form, both required payment in essence that couldn't be replaced, both risked consuming the practitioners who wielded such power.

"You murder people," she said, forcing her voice to remain steady despite the terror clawing at her chest. "You tear souls apart and weave them into weapons."

"Murder?" He laughed. "We preserve what others would let fade into nothing. Every echo in this chamber chose preservation over oblivion, accepted permanence despite the price required."

He gestured toward the bone walls, and the skin scrolls began to glow with increased intensity. Faces appeared in their phosphorescent text—not twisted by pain, but peaceful in ways that suggested acceptance.

"You heard the tapestry speak when you nearly bound those Memory Keeper voices to permanent form. You felt its hunger for more than stories, more than gentle reminiscence. It craved souls, threadbearer. Craved the complete essence of those who trusted you with their deepest memories."

The accusation struck her deeply because it carried a truth she'd been trying to ignore. The collective consciousness that had nearly claimed her hadn't been an accident or a mistake—it had been a natural progression of powers that grew stronger with each use, more demanding with each manifestation.

"That was different," she whispered. "I stopped before it went too far."

"Because you were afraid. Because you let sentiment override the logic of power." He rose from his chair and moved closer, close enough that she could smell decay beneath whatever perfumes he used to mask it. "But fear is a learned response, child. It can be unlearned when understanding replaces ignorance."

From beneath his robes, he withdrew a tapestry that made her scars burn with recognition. Not the twisted abominations she'd expected, but something that glowed with light similar to her own gift—threads worked with silver sigils.

"Behold our great work," he said with pride. "Every soul sacrificed for the greater good, every whisper of the past now serving a destiny beyond mortal comprehension. We are not destroyers. We are preservers, unbound by law and hypocrisy."

The tapestry's beauty struck a chord deep within her, vibrating through her bones like the first note of a forgotten song. She could feel the voices it contained—not screaming in agony but singing in harmonies too complex for mortal understanding. Each soul had willingly surrendered to this eternal chorus, exchanging the limitations of self for something vast and undying.

*Just like the spirits in my blood,* she thought with growing unease. *Just like what I almost became in the Memory Keepers' sanctuary.*

"You're trying to seduce me," she said, recognizing the manipulation even as part of her responded to its appeal. "Make me think we're similar, that your methods serve the same goals as mine."

"We are similar. Both of us understand that power requires sacrifice, that preservation demands payment in essence that can never be recovered. The only difference is my honesty about what that means."

He moved to another section of wall, where different tapestries hung like windows into scenes of carefully documented history. But these didn't show Wraithstitcher activities— they showed Guild operations, moments of official brutality that had been preserved for posterity.

"Watch," he commanded, activating the working had been woven into the fabric's patterns.

The visions that emerged made her stomach clench with revulsion. Guild soldiers burning libraries of preserved echoes, their fires consuming centuries of accumulated memory. Rogue weavers executed not for crimes they'd committed, but for abilities they possessed. Children whose gifts manifested early, disappearing into Guild custody and never seen again.

"They call us monsters," the Weaver said softly, his layered voice carrying sounds of genuine grief. "But we do not lie about our methods. We do not pretend our preservation comes without cost. When we take essence, we acknowledge the price and honor what we receive. The Guild simply destroys what they cannot control."

The moral equivalence he was drawing felt like poison, seductive in its logic but fundamentally corrupted. Yet she couldn't deny the evidence he'd shown her, couldn't dismiss the institutional brutality that had driven her into hiding in the first place.

*Is this what I would become if I stopped fighting the hunger?* she wondered. *Someone who rationalizes consumption as preservation, who transforms theft into honor?*

"I can see the doubt in your eyes," he continued, returning to his chair. "You understand now why we sought you out, why we preserved this sanctuary despite Guild and Memory Keeper interference. You are the threadbearer—the voice the stitches long for, the one who can bind echoes into perfect harmony."

"I won't help you." The words came out weaker than she'd intended, carrying uncertainty that undermined her defiant intent.

"Help us? Child, I am offering to help *you*." His laugh was genuinely delighted. "To teach you what your gift truly means, what it could accomplish if freed from artificial limitations. The Memory Keepers showed you preservation through partnership—but partnership requires consent, and the dead rarely consent to the uses the living require."

From another fold in his robes, he withdrew something that made her scars flare with painful recognition. A spool of thread that glowed with light similar to her own gift, but carrying frequencies that spoke of memories too precious to lose.

"A gift," he said, offering the spool with gesture that seemed genuinely generous. "No strings attached, no payment required. Simply an acknowledgment of what we share."

"What is it?" she asked, though part of her already knew.

"Your mother's final memory. The moment of your birth, when she held you for the first and last time before the fever took her." His voice carried sympathy that sounded authentic despite everything else about him. "A truth your grandmother kept from you out of misplaced protection, a connection that could be yours if you choose to stitch it yourself."

The temptation was overwhelming—not just the knowledge he offered, but the validation that came with it. Here was someone who understood her gift's true nature, who offered to teach rather than limit, who saw her potential as cause for celebration rather than fear.

"All power has cost, but not all cost is cruelty."

Her hands trembled as she reached toward the offered spool, her needle appearing without conscious thought. The memory-threads binding her arms burned with increased intensity, but they didn't prevent this movement—as if they recognized her mother's essence and chose not to interfere.

*One stitch*, she thought. *Just one, to learn the truth I've wondered about my entire life.*

But even as the rationalization formed, she understood what acceptance would mean. Not just knowledge, but the acknowledgment of kinship with someone who preserved memory through methods that violated everything she'd believed about consent and choice.

The needle trembled in her grip, poised between acceptance and rejection of knowledge that could transform everything she understood about herself. Around her, the Bone Cloister hummed with voices, all of them waiting to see whether she would join their eternal chorus or remain trapped in the limitations mortality imposed on those too afraid to embrace what they might become.

# CHAPTER 16
## Caedric

The sanctuary had become a graveyard. Caedric stood amid the smoldering ruins of what had been the Memory Keepers' hidden refuge, breathing air thick with smoke and the stench that came from supernatural corruption. Tapestries that had held centuries of wisdom lay in charred fragments, their silver threads dulled to ash while the echoes they'd contained dispersed into the darkness that awaited unbound spirits.

Bodies littered the chamber floor—Memory Keepers who'd died defending their life's work, Guild soldiers who'd discovered the Wraithstitchers weren't truly allies, cultists whose twisted forms had finally succumbed to wounds that leaked ichorous blood. The dead outnumbered the living by margins that spoke of a slaughter rather than a battle.

But it was the silence that truly marked the catastrophe. The tapestries that had once hummed with the wisdom of a thousand people now hung in tatters, their memories scattered like ashes on the wind, leaving behind a silence so complete it pressed against his eardrums like a physical weight. The sanctuary's protective weavings had unraveled under the assault, their enchantments dissolved by the corrupting touch of the Wraithstitchers.

*In all the noise of the battlefield, her voice was the one thread I couldn't let go of,* Caedric thought, replaying Amara's final scream as the Wraithstitchers dragged her into passages that led toward whatever hell they called home.

He'd failed her. Despite years of training, despite cutting every tie to his former life, despite promises that had felt like sacred oaths—when the moment came that mattered most, he'd been powerless to prevent her.

"This is your fault."

The accusation came from one of the surviving Memory Keepers whose robes were stained with blood that might have been his own or might have belonged to others. His young face was twisted with grief and rage that needed a target for the pain that threatened to consume him.

"If you hadn't brought the Guild's attention to our sanctuary, if you hadn't insisted on questioning our methods, if you'd simply trusted us to guide her properly—she'd still be here."

Other survivors gathered around the confrontation, their expressions ranging from sympathy to hostility. The unity that had once characterized the Memory Keepers had shattered like a mirror struck by stone, each shard reflecting a different truth about who had failed, who should answer for it, and which paths remained open to them now.

"The Guild was already watching," Caedric replied, his voice carrying steel despite the exhaustion that made every word an effort. "Your precious Serenya was feeding them information, coordinating this assault for reasons we may never understand. Amara was betrayed by someone she trusted, not by someone trying to protect her."

"Serenya is missing," said Lyra, an older woman whose scarred hands spoke of decades of working with dangerous threads. "Vanished during the fighting, along with several others whose loyalty was... questionable."

The confirmation of his suspicions brought no satisfaction, only bitter recognition that paranoia had been justified while trust had been fatal. The Memory Keepers had been compromised from within, their sanctuary transformed into a trap by people who'd spoken of preservation while planning destruction.

"Then we know who's responsible," the first continue, "But that doesn't explain why she went with them. Why she didn't fight harder, call upon the spirits in her blood for protection?"

"Maybe she did fight," snapped Rin, a young stitch-binder whose admiration for Amara had bordered on worship. "Maybe she fought until they overwhelmed her defenses and dragged her away unconscious."

"Or maybe she chose to go with them," said another voice from the gathered survivors. "Maybe the Weaver of Bone offered her something we couldn't."

The suggestion implied Amara wasn't a victim, but a willing collaborator. Caedric felt rage building in his chest, not just at the accusation, but at how easily these people who'd claimed to care about her were prepared to believe the worst when convenient explanations became necessary.

"She would never join them willingly," he said, his hand moving toward his thread-cutter though he stopped short of drawing the weapon. "Whatever else you believe about her choices, whatever doubts you harbor about her loyalty—she's not capable of the corruption that defines Wraithstitcher practice."

"Isn't she? You saw her nearly lose herself during the tapestry working. You witnessed how the voices in her blood grew stronger, more demanding, more willing to override her will. How do we know she hasn't already crossed lines we can't see?"

The question struck too close to the fears Caedric had been carrying since witnessing Amara's transformation after fleeing the Guild hall. Each use of her gift had pushed her further from normal humanity, each awakening of preserved voices had risked consuming whatever remained of her individual identity.

But crossing lines wasn't the same as choosing corruption. Transformation didn't necessarily mean surrendering to forces that would destroy everything she'd once valued.

*She's not one of them,* he told himself with conviction that felt like prayer. *Not yet. Not while there's still time to reach her before they complete whatever they've planned.*

———◆———

They found the wounded Wraithstitcher in one of the sanctuary's side chambers, half-buried under debris that had probably saved his life by concealing him from survivors seeking revenge. "Orem," he'd gasped when they dragged him into the lamplight. He was young by cultist standards, his face unmarked by the ritual scarification that characterized senior practitioners.

"Kill me," he whispered through lips cracked with dehydration and blood loss. "Please. I failed the Great Unraveling. I deserve only silence."

But Caedric had other plans for him. His robes were stitched with memory-threads that might contain useful information. Against the protests of Memory Keepers who wanted immediate execution, he placed his hands on fabric that reeked of supernatural corruption and opened his enhanced senses to whatever echoes the cloth might contain.

Memories spilled forth like broken glass—sharp-edged and incomplete, warped by the cultist's agony and the unnatural methods Wraithstitchers used to bind experiences to thread. Yet within the maelstrom, certain images crystallized with terrible clarity, filling him with equal measures of dread and desperate possibility.

Bone corridors carved with sigils. Chambers where tortured voices rose in harmonies too complex for the human throat. And through it all, a figure whose silver scars glowed with light that remained unbroken despite whatever bonds held her captive.

*Amara.*

"Bone Cloister," Orem whispered before consciousness fled entirely. "She goes to the Bone Cloister, where the Weaver waits to claim what has always been his."

The name meant nothing to most of the survivors, but Lyra's scarred face went pale with recognition. "The Bone Cloister is a legend. A place where the first Wraithstitchers learned to bind souls. If it truly exists..."

"Then that's where we'll find her," Caedric said. "Dead or alive, corrupted or pure—we'll bring her home."

The debate that followed revealed how thoroughly the Memory Keepers' unity had been shattered by the night's events. Some argued for an immediate rescue attempt, driven by loyalty to someone who'd trusted them with her transformation. Others insisted that pursuing Amara into Wraithstitcher territory was suicide that would accomplish nothing beyond adding their deaths to the night's toll.

Still others whispered that she might already be lost, claimed by the Wraithstitchers' infamous ability to twist even the purest souls into willing servants. Better to mourn her as a martyr than risk discovering she'd become something that required killing rather than saving.

"She's not lost," Caedric said, his voice cutting through their circular arguments. "Transformed, maybe. Changed by experiences none of us can fully understand, certainly. But not lost while she still breathes and thinks and chooses."

"And if she's chosen them?" someone asked. "If the Weaver of Bone has offered her everything we couldn't?"

"Then we'll remind her what she gave up to gain those things. We'll show her what corruption costs." Caedric's hand moved to his thread-cutter, its weight offering comfort that words couldn't provide. "But we won't abandon her to monsters because rescue seems too difficult."

The argument continued until dawn painted the sanctuary's ruins in shades of gold and crimson, but the outcome was never truly in doubt. Whatever divisions had emerged among the survivors, whatever doubts they harbored about Amara's loyalty or their chances of success—they couldn't simply abandon someone who'd become a symbol of resistance against the Guild's oppression.

A small team volunteered for what everyone understood might be a suicide mission. Lyra, whose tapestry scouting abilities could reveal paths through territories that remained invisible to ordinary senses. Iven, a gruff former Guild tailor whose knowledge of official techniques might prove useful against enemies who'd once served the same masters. Rin, the youngest among them, who tied memory-knots with more passion than precision but whose devotion to Amara burned bright enough to illuminate even the darkest corridors of doubt.

And Caedric, whose motivation was no longer about obligation, but had become something personal and deadly.

———◆———

As they prepared to depart the ruined sanctuary, Caedric found a message-stitch on his bedroll. It was made of thread from a Wraithstitcher's robe, woven into a pattern that formed two words: *Don't follow.*

The warning should have given him pause, should have raised questions about whether pursuit would endanger Amara further rather than providing rescue. Instead, it solidified his decision to go after her.

He held the message-thread over candle flame until it caught fire, watching silver light race along the weave like quicksilver before blackening to ash that crumbled away.

"Too late," he whispered. "Too late to turn back, too late to choose safety over loyalty, too late to pretend that losing you wouldn't destroy everything worth preserving in this broken world."

The small rescue party departed the sanctuary as the sun climbed toward its zenith, their packs heavy with supplies and weapons that might prove useless against their enemies. Behind them, the surviving Memory Keepers began the grim process of salvaging what could be saved while planning for a future that no longer included the sanctuary that had defined their purpose.

But ahead lay territory where normal rules held no meaning, where the Wraithstitchers had carved a kingdom from human suffering and called it paradise. The Bone Cloister waited somewhere in that wasteland, patient as death and twice as inevitable.

*The cult has taken her body, maybe even her will,* Caedric thought as they followed tracks that led toward a horizon painted in shades of despair. *But as long as I still carry her memory—I will not let them have her soul.*

# CHAPTER 17
## Amara

The chamber they'd given her was beautiful in the way that poisonous flowers were beautiful. Intricate, mesmerizing, and deadly. Bone lattice formed graceful arches overhead, each piece carved with sigils that pulsed with phosphorescent light. Between the bones, cloth stretched like skin across a framework of suffering, every thread soaked with memory-echoes that whispered constantly in languages she didn't recognize.

*They're trying to erode my thoughts,* she realized, pressing her palms against her ears in a futile attempt to block the voices. The stolen echoes would wear her down grain by grain, until her own voice became indistinguishable from the thousands they'd already harvested.

The memory-thread bindings were gone, leaving her physically free to move around the chamber's confines. But freedom meant little when the walls themselves were weapons designed to consume what remained of her. With each inhale, the murmurs of the damned filled her lungs; with each pulse, her blood seemed to flow in time with minds that had been captured against their will, forcing communion she had never consented to.

Food appeared at regular intervals, delivered by people that made her stomach lurch with revulsion. The whisper-servants moved without sound, their eyeless faces turned toward her with attention that felt like violation. They radiated silence so complete it seemed to absorb sound from the air around them, creating pockets of absolute quiet that were somehow more disturbing than the chamber's constant voices.

*They think taking away my tools means taking away my gift,* she thought, studying the servants.

Hidden beneath her fingernail, so small it was barely visible, lay single thread from the spool the Weaver of Bone had offered her.

She'd palmed it during their conversation, a reflex born from years of working with materials that wanted to be preserved rather than discarded. They'd searched her for weapons, for tools, for anything that might serve as focus for supernatural abilities.

But they hadn't thought to look for something as innocent as a hair's breadth of thread.

She began the work slowly, carefully, with movements so subtle they registered as nervous habits rather than purposeful activity. Amara traced patterns in the fabric of her own cloak—not cutting or tearing, but following existing seams with fingertip pressure that gradually worked the stolen thread into a new configuration.

Her breath became a tool as vital as any needle, carrying intent that shaped reality according to her will rather than physical manipulation. This was the ancient way, from before the Guild's scrolls and formal instruction, when weavers first learned to listen to what thread wanted to become. Not mastery over material, but conversation—a whispered exchange between fingers and fiber that honored both voices equally.

Beneath her fingertips, threads shifted into a pattern older than language—three intersecting curves that folded inward like a secret kept willingly. Not the rigid silence of the voiceless, but the powerful quiet of one who knows when to withhold truth from those who would weaponize it. The stitch sapped strength from her bones, draining vitality she could ill spare, yet it proved that her captors' control was less absolute than they believed.

The first victory was silencing a section of wall that had been particularly aggressive in its whispering. Not destroying the voices— that would have been noticed immediately— but convincing them to focus their attention elsewhere, to seek easier prey among those less prepared for their assault.

The second was learning to read the seams of her captors' robes when they visited her chamber. Memory-threads worked into fabric carried information about the Bone Cloister's layout, about passages that led toward the surface, about weaknesses in the weavings that kept this place hidden from external detection.

But the most important victory was the gradual unraveling of concealment magic that cloaked the entire complex from outside observation. Thread by careful thread, she loosened the bindings that maintained the Cloister's invisibility, creating hairline fractures through which messages might escape.

"You're adapting well."

The voice belonged to Veyra, a mute Wraithstitcher whose scarred throat spoke of surgical removal rather than an accident or disease. She communicated through hand gestures and fabric manipulation, her robes worked with threads that glowed when she needed to convey complex concepts.

"The others expected you to break within days," Veyra continued, her hands shaping words from silk that appeared and dissolved like smoke. "The whispers usually consume new arrivals before they can establish proper defenses. But you've learned to deflect rather than resist. Interesting."

Amara said nothing, though she filed the information away for future reference. They'd built this chamber not as a cage for her body but as a labyrinth for her mind, expecting her thoughts to unravel thread by thread until nothing remained but echoes of what she had been.

But silence apparently conveyed its own information. Veyra's eyeless face turned toward the section of wall Amara had quieted, then back to her with what might have been approval.

"The Weaver of Bone wishes to speak with you again."

——◆——

He entered with the same unsettling presence as before, but this time he carried curiosity rather than hunger. The obsidian needle in his hands gleamed with malevolent light that made her scars burn with responding fire.

"You've been busy," he said, his layered voice carrying sounds of genuine amusement. "Subtle work, skillfully done. Most of our guests are too busy screaming to attempt such creative applications of their abilities."

The needle extended toward her like an offering, its point sharp enough to draw blood from unwary handling. "All we ask is that you record one stitch, one memory, one honest account of yourself."

Trap. The word blazed across her consciousness like a warning written in fire. The needle would record whatever memories she accessed while using it, would transfer her thoughts directly into the tapestry the cult used to preserve their trophies. One careless stitch, and her entire history would become their property.

But her refusal would confirm their suspicions about her secret activities, would probably lead to closer confinement and the end of the opportunities that remained for escape or rescue.

"Very well," she said, accepting the needle. "But I choose which memory to preserve."

His laugh was a sound like wind stirring dried leaves, carrying a satisfaction that suggested her compliance had been anticipated and prepared for.

"Of course. We are not monsters. We understand the value of choice, the importance of voluntary participation in great workings." He gestured toward fabric that hung from the chamber's ceiling. "Simply touch the needle to cloth and let your chosen memory flow in. Nothing more complex than what you've done countless times before."

He left her alone with the obsidian needle and the blank fabric that waited for the story she chose to tell. Amara considered her limited options. The Wraithstitchers expected compliance, but they'd given her a tool that could serve her in ways they hadn't anticipated.

Instead of recording her own memories, she began working a reverse echo into the tapestry's threads, a pattern that would ripple outward—a beacon that might penetrate the walls that held her captive, carrying whispers of her presence to those who might be listening beyond.

The technique was theoretical, something she'd read about in her grandmother's notes but never attempted.

Theoretical until now.

The obsidian needle sang through the cloth, each stitch carrying power that made her fingertips burn with more than simple threadburn. But instead of drawing memory from her consciousness into permanent form, she pushed fragments of herself outward—location, condition, desperate hope that someone was listening for such signals.

*I don't need to scream,* she thought, watching patterns take shape that begged for rescue and stressed urgency. *I need to stitch.*

Each knot proved that communication was possible despite the barriers designed to prevent it. The reverse echo built slowly, carefully, charged with intention rather than mere information. And then, as she completed the final connection between broadcast threads and the network of memory that connected all fabric across vast distances, her scars blazed with silver fire that painted the chamber walls in shifting patterns.

The sensation was unmistakable—consciousness touching the other end of her desperate message, recognition flowing back along pathways that connected every weaver to every other weaver regardless of distance or obstacle.

*Coming.*

The word formed in her mind with clarity, carrying echoes of a familiar voice despite the supernatural medium through which it traveled. Someone had received her signal, understood its implications, committed to action despite the dangers such commitment entailed.

The recognition brought tears to her eyes—not just relief at successful contact, but overwhelming gratitude that someone cared enough to risk everything for her protection.

She set the obsidian needle aside and studied the tapestry she'd created, noting how its reverse echo patterns had been seamlessly integrated into the preservation the Wraithstitchers had expected. To casual observation, it would appear she'd complied with their demands for recorded memory while concealing the true nature of her working.

*They thought they'd buried me in silence,* she thought, watching silver light fade from the threads that now hummed with purpose. *But even buried, thread finds thread. And I am not done weaving.*

Outside her chamber, the Bone Cloister continued its eternal whispers—tortured voices calling for mercy that would never come, echoes bound to purposes they'd never chosen. But now those whispers carried different harmonies, frequencies that spoke of hope rather than despair.

Rescue was coming. The only question was whether she would remain herself long enough to recognize salvation when it arrived, or whether the constant pressure of stolen echoes would finally succeed in eroding what remained of her mind.

# CHAPTER 18
## Caedric

The Bone Wastes stretched before them like a wound carved into the world's flesh—ash-colored dunes that shifted in the wind, fossilized remains jutting from earth that had forgotten how to nurture life. Three days of travel through increasingly desolate terrain had brought Caedric's small rescue party to the edge of territory that appeared on no Guild maps, a place where even cartographers feared to venture.

*No wonder the Wraithstitchers chose this for their stronghold,* Caedric thought, studying the horizon that seemed to bend light in directions that made his eyes water. *A land so cursed that even the desperate avoid it.*

Their camp huddled in the lee of calcified ribs that might once have belonged to some enormous beast, the bones providing shelter from winds that carried whispers in languages long forgotten. Lyra sat across from their small fire, her scarred hands working threads through a veil that allowed her to perceive supernatural currents invisible to normal sight.

"Something's changed," she said suddenly, her enhanced senses picking up disturbances that made her entire body tense with alertness. "There's a ripple in the weave, coming from deeper in the Wastes."

She pressed the stitched veil closer to her face, her breathing becoming shallow as her concentration deepened. Around them, the air itself seemed to thicken with supernatural tension, reality bending under pressure.

"It's her," Lyra whispered, her voice carrying awe mixed with terror. "Amara. She's... she's broadcasting. A reverse echo, impossibly complex, threaded through strong barriers. I'm surprised she penetrated through them."

Caedric felt his heart skip several beats as understanding crashed over him like cold water. "Can you read the message?"

"Fragments. The signal's degrading over distance, and whatever's generating interference..." She pressed harder, then jerked back with cry of pain that sent blood streaming from her nose. "She's alive. Conscious. And asking for help."

The confirmation brought relief so intense it left him momentarily dizzy, only to be replaced by determination that burned like a forge fire in his chest. Amara wasn't just surviving whatever the Wraithstitchers had planned, she was fighting back, using abilities they probably didn't realize she possessed.

*Hold on,* he projected toward the connection. *I'm coming.*

———◆———

Dawn brought no improvement to the landscape's terrain. If anything, daylight revealed details that darkness had mercifully concealed—bone fragments embedded in every surface, ash that moved like living things when disturbed, and the persistent sense of being observed by eyes that belonged to consciousness long since departed.

"The Bone Wastes are cursed," Iven said, his gruff voice carrying the reluctance that had been building since they'd entered this desolate territory. "Not just dangerous, actively malevolent. The magic here has been twisted by whatever catastrophe created this place."

Rin nodded agreement, her young face pale with the strain of maintaining basic protective wards against the energy that pressed against them from every direction. "My stitch-bindings keep unraveling on their own. It's like the land itself rejects any attempt at normal weaving."

*They're right,* Caedric realized as he studied the way shadows fell at angles that defied the sun's position. This wasn't simply a wasteland—it was a territory where the rules of reality had been damaged beyond repair, leaving ragged edges where nightmares could slip through into the waking world.

*No wonder Guild records contained no detailed surveys of this region. Anyone who ventured too deep probably never returned to file reports.*

But retreat wasn't an option, not with Amara's signal growing stronger as they pushed deeper into terrain that seemed designed to drive intruders mad. They pressed forward through dunes that whispered with the voices of those who'd died here, past ruins of settlements where only foundation stones remained, silent witnesses to calamities that had consumed all who might have told their stories.

The attack came without warning.

The Echo Storm rose from the ground, tattered remnants of clothing long abandoned, now twisting and spiraling through the air as if possessed by vengeful spirits. Shreds of cloth danced in the air, their memory-threads cut loose from their makers' intent. Years of solitude in this forsaken place had twisted them, transformed into weapons that sought only to inflict the suffering they'd absorbed.

Overlapping voices filled the air until rational thought became impossible—screams of battle victims mixed with the laughter of celebrating children, war chants blended with funeral dirges, words of tenderness corrupted into vile oaths that seemed to make the very air recoil from their utterance.

*The threads aren't just unraveling,* Caedric realized as he threw up a binding weave to hold his companions together. *They're trying to pull us into the past, to make us part of whatever tragedy created this place.*

The effort of maintaining protective barriers left his hands shredded and bleeding, silver light from his thread-cutter the only thing preventing complete dissolution into the chaos that surrounded them. Beside him, Lyra screamed as phantom needles worked patterns in her flesh, while Rin sobbed with grief that belonged to someone else's memories.

Only Iven remained unaffected, his older techniques apparently offering protection against the forces that fed on emotional resonance. "Don't let them in!" he shouted over the supernatural cacophony. "The echoes want to live again—they'll use your bodies if you give them purchase!"

The storm raged, stretching and compressing moments like fabric under a tailor's hands. In this broken place, time flowed like thread through a crooked needle—sometimes bunching, sometimes pulling taut, never following the straight line of minutes that governed the world. But eventually the fragments settled back to earth, their animate fury exhausted by the effort of manifesting so far from the sources had originally charged them with purpose.

When silence finally returned, it felt like a blessing from gods who'd abandoned hope for mortal survival.

"I can't go further," Iven announced that evening, his weathered face showing defeat that had nothing to do with physical exhaustion. "This place... I've seen it before. In Guild records that were supposed to be destroyed, reports of operations that officially never happened."

He gestured toward bone-markers that had begun appearing along their path—totems constructed from human remains. Each one carried messages stitched in hair and sinew, warnings written in materials that had once been living flesh.

"This was a purge site," he continued, his voice barely above a whisper. "Somewhere the Guild brought problems they couldn't solve through normal channels. Entire communities of practitioners, eliminated so thoroughly that their existence was erased from historical record."

The final marker they encountered held a message that chilled Caedric's blood despite the day's oppressive heat: *Last warning*. The words were worked in what looked like children's hair, their innocent origins making the threat feel obscene rather than simply dangerous.

"I won't be party to whatever lies beyond this point," Iven said, shouldering his pack, his decision made. "Some places are cursed for good reason. Some doors should remain closed."

Caedric watched the older man depart with understanding if not approval. The Bone Wastes had revealed their true nature. It wasn't simply a dangerous territory, but a graveyard where Guild authority had written history in blood and bone before erasing its own participation. Only those who had severed all ties to Guild oaths could bear to tread further.

For Caedric, Guild loyalty was a currency whose value had depreciated beyond recognition.

———◆———

Alone by their fire after Rin had followed Iven's example and departed for safer ground, Caedric found himself remembering the first time he'd seen Amara. Not the official interrogation in the Guild Hall, but the moment when she'd emerged from her basement room to find him waiting in shadows between buildings.

The fear in her gold-flecked eyes hadn't been directed at him personally—she hadn't known his purpose. But she'd recognized authority in his bearing, had understood immediately that her quiet life of mending torn cloth was about to end in ways she couldn't control.

*She was always more than a target,* he thought, watching flames dance across the meager pile of wood they had found. *Even before I knew her name, before I understood what she could become, there was something about her that made simple duty feel inadequate.*

The Guild had trained him to see people like her as problems requiring solution, threats to be neutralized before they could damage the careful balance that kept magical power from consuming civilization. But Amara had never felt threatening in ways that mattered. Her gift served compassion rather than ambition.

If the Guild's authority rested on preventing such practitioners from existing freely, then perhaps that authority deserved whatever challenges it faced.

Morning brought Lyra's quiet announcement that she could sense the Bone Cloister's presence—not the location exactly, but a distortion in the air where decades of pain had been mortared between stones like a poisonous grout. They were close now, close enough that her enhanced senses could detect the massive workings that kept the Wraithstitchers' stronghold hidden from casual observation.

The chasm appeared without warning, a crack in the earth's surface that descended into darkness deeper than natural caves should allow. But instead of empty space, the opening was sealed by a weaving so complex it made Caedric's vision blur—thousands of threads worked into patterns that held stone and shadow in configurations that defied physical law.

"That's not Wraithstitcher work," Lyra said, studying the barrier. "The techniques are too gentle."

Caedric moved closer, analyzing the power that held the entrance closed. Beneath the complexity, he found something that made his chest tighten with recognition—frequencies that resonated with silver scars he'd learned to associate with one particular weaver.

"It's hers," he said, understanding flooding through him like revelation. "Amara sealed this entrance. Not to keep us out, but to keep them in."

She wasn't just surviving captivity, she was actively working to contain the Wraithstitchers, using her abilities to turn their own stronghold into a prison rather than a sanctuary.

But the barrier was failing. He could see threads beginning to fray under pressure from what lay beneath, could hear voices rising from the depths that should have remained forever silent. Whatever Amara had accomplished, it wouldn't hold much longer.

"Help me," he said to Lyra, drawing his thread-cutter while she prepared her tools. "We need to unweave this carefully. Maintain the binding while creating passage for two people."

The work required precision that left no room for error or hesitation. Each severed thread had to be replaced immediately with new weaving that preserved the barrier's essential function while allowing limited access. Gradually, thread by careful thread, an opening large enough for human passage began to take shape.

*Hold on, Amara,* Caedric thought. *I'm coming for you.* He took a final breath of surface air and stepped into the darkness that hummed with tormented voices.

# CHAPTER 19
## Amara

The chamber they brought her to felt different from the bone-latticed cell that had been her prison. It was larger, more ornate. Tapestries covered every surface, their threads worked with materials that made her recoil in disgust. Not just memory-threads, but something darker—pain given form, suffering compressed into silk that whispered with the voices of those who'd died in agony.

"You have earned freedom of movement," the Weaver of Bone announced. "A reward for compliance, a recognition of growing understanding between kindred spirits."

But Amara recognized the calculated nature of his generosity. The chamber's boundaries were marked by wards she could perceive but not cross, invisible barriers that would contain her just as effectively as physical walls. This wasn't freedom—it was a larger cage designed to create the illusion of trust while maintaining absolute control.

"Your next task," he continued, gesturing toward the oldest tapestry in the collection, "is interpretation. This working predates the founding of our order, woven by one whose madness exceeded mortal understanding. He glimpsed a truth others fear to acknowledge."

The ancient textile's patterns shifted between configurations that seemed to depict different possible futures. Bone thread had been worked into its weave—not decoratively, but structurally, creating framework that held visions in suspension like insects trapped in amber.

It was both an offer and a threat, she realized. Translate it, or become part of it.

The cult's magic operated on principles that turned everything she'd learned about weaving inside out. Where her techniques sought harmony between practitioner and material, theirs imposed dominance through suffering. Where she preserved voices that chose to be remembered, they harvested echoes from souls that had been tortured until consent became meaningless. But underneath the corruption lay methods she could understand and, more importantly, subvert.

Their spells bound not just body but belief. She discovered this while studying the ceremonial robes worn by junior cultists. Threads of echoed pain were woven into garments that convinced their wearers that the cult's version of reality was the only truth worth accepting. Doubt, hope, individual will—all of it gradually eroded by the constant exposure to voices that spoke only of submission and despair.

*They stitch fate itself into the fabric,* she realized with growing horror. *They convince their followers that resistance is impossible because their threads say so.*

But if threads could carry such messages, they could also carry others. Working in stolen moments when no one observed her directly, Amara began practicing reverse applications of the techniques she'd decoded from the cult's workings. Not binding belief, but loosening it. Not reinforcing despair, but sowing seeds of doubt that might eventually grow into rebellion.

The first test came when she found a loose thread in one of the chamber's wall hangings—a silver strand that had worked free from the pattern that held the others captive. Instead of tucking it back into place, she used it to send another encoded signal beyond the Cloister's barriers.

Not a cry for help this time, but a warning: *They see everything. Don't trust the cloth.*

The message carried urgency born from understanding how thoroughly the cult's influence extended. If Caedric was truly coming for her—and every instinct said he was—he needed to know that normal caution might not be sufficient against enemies who could weave deception into the very fabric of reality.

Her first act of sabotage was subtle enough to pass unnoticed among people who expected absolute obedience from their followers. A ceremonial robe worn by one of the junior Wraithstitchers, its hem worked with sigils that reinforced loyalty and suppressed individual thought. It was a simple matter of altering a single character in the pattern, changing a rune of obedience to one of echo reflection.

The effect was immediate and devastating. Instead of hearing the cult's reinforcing whispers, the wearer began experiencing their own forgotten memories—fragments of the person they'd been before joining the order of madness. Childhood laughter, moments of genuine happiness, love that had existed before being corrupted into a weapon.

The breakdown was spectacular. Screaming, convulsions, desperate pleas for the voices to stop speaking truths that had been buried under years of indoctrination. But the other cultists interpreted the episode as spiritual testing rather than sabotage, evidence that their colleague was being purified through sacred suffering.

Amara remained above suspicion while watching her first victim carried away to whatever treatment the cult provided for those whose faith wavered.

*If I can rewrite one robe, I can rewrite them all,* she thought, studying the other garments with new understanding of their vulnerabilities.

"You show remarkable aptitude for our methods," the Weaver of Bone said when he summoned her again, his attention focused on the progress she'd made interpreting the ancient prophecy tapestry. "You grasp intuitively what others struggle for decades to comprehend—the malleability of what people call truth, how it can be stitched into whatever design best serves those who control the needle."

The words slithered from his lips like venomous flattery, confirming her worst fear—that she had absorbed precisely the knowledge he'd intended her to gain. Yet his eyes narrowed slightly when she nodded, the subtle tension in his shoulders betraying suspicion that her obedience might be performance rather than conversion.

"There was another, once," he continued, settling into a chair that creaked with the sounds of settling bone. "A girl much like you, gifted with abilities that exceeded normal understanding. She came to us willingly, seeking the knowledge we possessed about the deeper applications of memory-weaving."

The story that followed was clearly intended as a warning disguised as history, but Amara leaned forward slightly, her fingers unconsciously tracing patterns on her knee as she absorbed every word with the intensity of a weaver memorizing a forbidden pattern.

"She learned our techniques with remarkable speed, showed such promise that we considered elevating her to positions of true authority within our order. But pride corrupted her judgment, convinced her that she could improve upon methods perfected through centuries of careful experimentation."

His layered voice dropped to a whisper that somehow carried more menace than shouting would have. "She thought resistance could be quiet, sabotage subtle enough to escape our notice. But silence does not protect anyone from the needle. We wove her mind into bindings that holds this very chamber together—she lives on, whispering madness through the seams of the Cloister."

Amara forced her expression to remain neutral despite the chill that ran down her spine. Around them, the tapestry-lined walls seemed to pulse with responding rhythm, as if an invisible presence was acknowledging the truth of his words.

*Is she still here?* she wondered. *Still conscious, still suffering, transformed into an architectural element but retaining enough awareness to understand what she's become?*

"I show no fear because there is nothing to fear from the truth," she said aloud, meeting his gaze with a steadiness that felt more like a performance. "Your methods preserve what would otherwise be lost. That some pay prices others consider excessive is unfortunate but necessary."

His smile revealed he was genuinely pleased, suggesting her response had passed whatever test he'd intended. After he left, her hands trembled as she realized that only a thread's width separated her fate from that of the girl woven into the walls.

———◆———

The ancient prophecy tapestry revealed its secrets slowly, grudgingly, like a puzzle designed to frustrate rather than illuminate. But gradually, patterns emerged from the chaos—not just visions of possible futures, but a map worked into the weave's foundation with skill that transcended artistry.

The layout matched portions of the Guild Hall in Deymar, corridors and chambers she vaguely found familiar from her desperate flight. But this version showed modifications—additional passages, structural changes, preparation for something that required access to places normally sealed against intrusion.

*A siege,* she realized. *They're planning an assault on the Guild Hall itself.*

Whatever alliance that existed between the cult and the Guild, whatever cooperation had allowed the coordinated attack on the Memory Keepers' sanctuary, it must have been a temporary arrangement designed to serve larger purposes neither side had revealed to the other.

But worse than strategic betrayal was the personal threat she discovered stitched beneath the architectural plans. A symbol worked in the threads that pulsed with malevolent intent, surrounded by patterns that spoke of binding and consumption and permanent silence.

Caedric's name, rendered in script that made her scars burn with sympathetic fire.

*They mean to stitch his death into history.*

The prophecy didn't just predict his demise—it was designed to ensure it, channeling the collective will of countless believers to bend reality to serve the cult's vision.

Working with desperate speed that left her fingers bloody and her vision blurred with exhaustion, Amara began unraveling portions of the ancient tapestry. Not destruction for its own sake, but careful replacement of key elements with alternatives that served different purposes.

Where the original had woven Caedric's death into inevitable fate, she stitched survival despite impossible odds. Where it had depicted the Guild Hall falling, she crafted images of resistance that grew stronger rather than weaker under pressure.

Most importantly, where it had prophesied cult victory through superior understanding, she wove their downfall through hubris that made them blind to threats they'd created through their own actions.

The false prophecy that emerged wasn't masterwork—she lacked both time and resources for truly convincing forgery. But it planted seeds of doubt about outcomes the cult had assumed were guaranteed, suggestions that their planned assault might face complications their visions hadn't anticipated.

*Let them wonder,* she thought, studying her work with satisfaction. *Let them question whether their threads truly show fate or merely wishful thinking.*

Around her, the Bone Cloister hummed with the voices of those who'd been consumed by cult ideology. But now those voices carried different harmonies. Uncertainty where once there'd been conviction, questions where once there'd been absolute answers.

*They want me to be a seamstress of memory,* she thought, watching the silver light fade from the threads that would carry her subtle rebellion into the future the cult sought to create. *They will regret every thread I touch.*

The war for her soul was far from over, but she was no longer fighting defensively. Each day brought new opportunities for sabotage, new chances to turn the cult's own methods against the certainties that held their order together.

And somewhere beyond the Cloister's barriers, help was coming. She could feel it. The Weaver of Bone thought he'd claimed another vessel for his accumulated madness. Instead, he'd acquired an enemy who understood his methods well enough to corrupt them from within.

The only question was whether her rebellion would bear fruit before the cult completed the ritual they'd planned.

# CHAPTER 20
## Caedric

Caedric's thread-cutter caught the cultist's barbed needle mid-thrust. The Wraithstitcher hissed, a sound that held too many voices, and yanked back, preparing for another strike.

"Left!" Lyra's warning came just in time. Caedric pivoted as a second attacker emerged from the shadows. His blade sang through the air, severing the connections between the cultist's weapon and the tortured memories that powered it. The figure crumpled, its robes dissolving into component threads.

Three more sentries materialized from alcoves Caedric hadn't noticed in the dim light. These underground passages were a maze of defensive positions, each one designed to funnel intruders into killing zones. Guild training had taught him to recognize such architecture, but knowing the trap existed didn't make it any easier to avoid.

Beside him, Lyra's mirrored veil blazed with reflected light as she deflected a barrage of needle-strikes. The technique required perfect timing—catch the attack in the veil's surface, reflect it back before the supernatural energy could take hold. One mistake and those barbed tips would pierce not just flesh, but memory itself, unraveling her sense of self thread by thread.

"The corridor narrows ahead," she gasped, maintaining her defensive barrier while tracking enemy movements. "We'll be trapped if more come from behind."

Caedric drove forward, forcing the remaining sentries to give ground. His thread-cutter found the binding points in their defensive wards, each severed connection releasing voices that had been compressed into barriers—tortured fragments that screamed as they dissipated. The sound made his teeth ache, but he didn't slow. Hesitation meant death.

The last cultist fell, and suddenly the passage was silent except for their ragged breathing.

"The main corridor is clear," Lyra whispered, her voice carrying the strain from maintaining the veil. "But I can feel deeper workings stirring. They're planning something, and it's already begun."

Walls stretched upward into darkness beyond the reach of their conjured light, their surfaces covered in tapestries that writhed with captured screams. The weavings depicted scenes of agony, each stitch a compressed fragment of the moment when hope had died in someone's eyes. Caedric had seen death in many forms during his years with the Hemlock Circle, but this was different. This was death prolonged, forced to relive its final moments endlessly.

Lyra gasped beside him. "How many souls are trapped here?"

Caedric didn't answer. He was counting the tapestries—twelve visible from where they stood, but the chamber extended into shadows that suggested dozens, if not hundreds, more. His thread-cutter hummed with residual energy from the sentries they'd dispatched. The blade's silver glow seemed dimmer here, as if the chamber's darkness was actively consuming light. He adjusted his grip, acutely aware that every second they spent in this place increased the risk of discovery.

"The working you sensed," he said quietly. "Can you pinpoint its source?"

Lyra closed her eyes, her breathing slowing as she extended her awareness. The technique was dangerous—opening oneself to supernatural currents while surrounded by hostile magic—but they had no other means of navigation in this labyrinth of corruption.

After a moment that stretched too long for Caedric's comfort, her eyes snapped open. "Deeper. There's a central chamber below this one, and the power emanating from it..." She paused, and he saw fear flash across her features. "Whatever they're creating down there, it's massive. I've never felt anything like it."

They moved deeper into the fortress, leaving the bodies behind. The passage descended in a gentle slope, and instead of a rough cavern, they entered what appeared to be a cathedral. Walls stretched upward into darkness beyond the reach of the light, and at the chamber's heart, the Weaver of Bone stood before a tapestry unlike anything he'd seen before.

Ancient patterns worked with bone thread and worse materials, their designs shifting between configurations that seemed to depict different possible futures. But the tapestry wasn't merely predicting the future—it was weaving it, thread by thread, bending the fabric of existence to match some incomprehensible design that no human mind was meant to fathom.

"Behold the culmination of centuries of careful preparation," the Weaver intoned, his layered voice vibrating through Caedric's bones like fingers stroking the inside of his skull. "The Guild's memory-web, exposed and vulnerable, ready for surgical modification that will serve our greater purposes."

Behind him, barely visible in ceremonial robes that disguised her familiar form, Amara stood with her head bowed in apparent submission. But Caedric caught a glimpse of silver light beneath the dark fabric, scars that pulsed with their own rhythm despite whatever bonds held her captive.

*She's still fighting,* he realized, a wave of hope washing through him that almost drowned out his combat instincts. *Still herself.*

The ritual tapestry showed Deymar in minute detail—not just physical structures, but the supernatural networks that connected every Guild facility to the Pattern Council's central authority. And woven through those connections, like an infection spreading through healthy tissue, were modifications designed to erase the city's existence from magical record entirely.

But worse than that was the personal threat he recognized in the pattern's deeper layers. His own thread worked into the design, encircled by runes of imprisonment and soul-devouring sigils.

*My death is required for the working to complete,* he understood.

Their sudden appearance shattered the concentration the ritual required. Wraithstitchers spun toward them with inhuman speed, but Amara was faster. Her blade—not steel, but something that gleamed with light similar to her scars—slashed diagonally across the ritual tapestry. The cut wasn't random vandalism but precise and targeted, severing connections that held the working's most crucial elements together.

The backlash was immediate and catastrophic. Threads that had been forced into unnatural configurations snapped back toward equilibrium, their released tension creating shock waves that made the chamber's bone architecture groan with stress. Reality itself seemed to flinch away from patterns that had been designed to violate its fundamental nature.

Time suspended itself as Caedric found Amara's gaze across the unraveling chamber. Despite everything, she remained recognizably herself. The gold flecks in her brown eyes still held defiance rather than surrender, determination rather than despair.

Then the Wraithstitchers attacked, and the moment of recognition dissolved into the chaos of combat. But this time, he wasn't fighting alone. Amara's abilities pushed beyond normal limits, her improvised blade cutting through enemy manifestations while her free hand worked threads that called spectral defenders from the remnants of power still accessible in the chamber.

They fought as partners rather than protector and protected, each covering weaknesses the other couldn't address. Her gift provided supernatural support while his training offered tactical expertise, their combined abilities proving more effective than either could have achieved alone.

"Enough."

The Weaver of Bone's voice cut through the combat like a blade through silk, carrying power that made every thread in the chamber vibrate with responding frequency. When he raised his needle, reality bent around its point in ways that made rational thought difficult.

"You dare pit yourself against knowledge refined across a thousand lifetimes?" Laughter rippled beneath his words. "You play at power like infants with toys, while I command forces that were ancient when your Guild was nothing but a whisper in the void."

The needle swept toward Lyra with speed that surpassed physical motion, its barbed point seeking connection with the threads that held her identity together. When it found purchase, she screamed—not with physical agony but the primal horror of watching her own essence unravel.

*He's not just killing her*, Caedric realized with horror. *He's unraveling who she is, pulling apart the threads that make her an individual person.*

Lyra's eyes went blank as memories dissolved, her mouth working soundlessly around a name she could no longer recall. The mirror-veil fell from nerveless fingers as the tapestry of her being scattered like morning mist.

The Weaver pivoted toward Caedric, his ancient needle poised to unpick the very threads of his existence, but before it could find purchase, a silver thread coiled around his wrist like liquid moonlight. Not a restraint, but a shield.

Amara's voice rose above the din, and the protective stitch she'd bound around his wrist blazed with light that made the Weaver recoil, his needle unable to penetrate the barrier.

"You want echoes?" she said, her voice rattling the chamber's bone walls. "Here's mine."

Caedric watched in awe as Amara's power manifested in ways that defied everything he thought he'd learned about her abilities. This was no gentle calling of ancestral whispers, no coaxing of cooperative phantoms. This was primordial magic that bridged the vast chasms between souls, reaching across the boundaries that kept each consciousness distinct and separate from all others.

A soul-link. Realization struck him like a thunderbolt. Amara was redirecting the hungry pattern back toward its source, forcing the ancient collector to taste his own dissolution as the stolen identities he'd woven into himself began to unravel at their seams.

Centuries of stolen voices erupted from the Weaver's form as carefully maintained barriers dissolved. His scream contained multitudes—every soul he'd tormented, every echo he'd bound, every fragment of consciousness he'd claimed for his collection.

But the effort was draining Amara. Blood streamed from her nose and fingertips while silver light from her scars grew dim. Each thread she pulled exacted its toll in lifeforce, draining her until she stood hollow as an empty loom.

The Bone Cloister's collapse began with sounds like breaking glass multiplied a thousandfold. The chamber's architecture began to unravel—bone-white pillars crumbling like ancient teeth, arcane bindings unspooling from the ceiling in gossamer strands that disintegrated before touching the floor. Each crack that formed released a whisper of spent magic, the sound like silk tearing across an infinite loom.

"We need to leave," Caedric shouted over the cacophony of destruction, seizing Lyra's arm as she gazed vacantly at the disintegrating chamber, her eyes hollow of any recognition. "Now, before the whole structure comes down!"

They fled through corridors where walls buckled and twisted, the once-solid architecture dissolving as threads pulled free from their bindings like sutures from living flesh. Behind them, the cultists fled in all directions, some melting into threads of their own creation as the protective enchantments that had preserved their unnatural existence unraveled into nothingness.

Amara staggered beside him, her breathing ragged with exhaustion that went deeper than physical fatigue. The soul-link had pushed her abilities beyond any safe limit, demanding a price that might take years to fully understand.

———◆———

Moonlight had never felt so beautiful as when they finally emerged from the passages that led toward surface air. Behind them, the Bone Cloister collapsed, its twisted architecture folding in upon itself like a dying spider, destined to be swallowed by the hungry earth of this blighted realm.

Lyra sat on a fallen stone, her hands pressed to her temples. When she looked up, tears streamed down her cheeks.

"You saved me," she whispered, her voice carrying awe mixed with gratitude. "Both of you. I don't remember everything that happened, but I remember that."

Caedric knelt beside Amara, his gaze tracing the silvery fluid that seeped from beneath her skin and mingled with her blood. The soul-link had carved channels in her essence that would probably never fully heal, a permanent reminder of what she had sacrificed so others might live.

"Why didn't you wait for rescue?" he asked, beginning the limited field treatment his supplies could provide.

"Because sometimes the only way out is to tear the seams yourself." Weariness threaded through her words, yet beneath it ran a current of fierce pride—the kind that comes only from defying the patterns others have laid out and weaving one's own design instead. "I couldn't risk them completing the ritual, couldn't let them rewrite reality."

She was right, he knew. The Weaver's working would have eliminated Deymar from magical records, erasing centuries of history because it conflicted with cult ideology. But what she'd done went beyond averting disaster—she had kept the world a place where people could still choose their own fates rather than have them dictated by ancient powers and their self-appointed interpreters.

As he worked to clean and bind her wounds, Amara's voice dropped to a whisper. "There's more. The map I saw in their prophecy tapestry... Deymar wasn't the only city marked for elimination."

The implication settled in his chest like lead. They'd prevented immediate disaster, but a larger plot remained.

"The cult wasn't destroyed," she continued, her eyes burning with an intensity that rivaled the stars above them. "Just stitched deeper into the world. And I think... I think I'm still connected to their leader. The soul-link didn't just turn his spell against him—it bound us together."

*The Weaver of Bone lives*, Caedric realized. *Wounded, diminished, but alive and now magically tethered to the woman who defeated him.*

The war for her soul was far from over. If anything, her victory had created new complications that would require solutions neither of them possessed yet. But it had been her decision, and as long as she was free to choose her own path, he would stand beside her.

The night sky stretched above them, countless stars glittering with ancient light. The universe continued its vast, indifferent dance while below, three figures huddled close, their breathing synchronized in the quiet aftermath of choices that had nearly cost them everything.

The journey continues with...
Threads of War

# About the Author

Richard Fierce is a fantasy author with a passion for storytelling that dates back to his childhood. He first ventured into publishing in 2007 and hasn't looked back since. His books are filled with dragons, adventure, and the kind of epic journeys that transport readers to new worlds.

In 2000, Richard was named Poet of the Year for his poem The Darkness, and his love for literature extends beyond just writing—he co-founded the Acworth Book Festival in Georgia to help bring authors and readers together. Though he originally worked in retail, he eventually transitioned to the tech industry, balancing his career with his writing.

Richard lives in Northwest Georgia with his family and a lively mix of pets, including four dogs (huskies!). He often jokes that his house feels like a zoo, but he wouldn't have it any other way.

His love for fantasy started in high school when he was gifted a copy of *Dragons of Spring Dawning* by Margaret Weis and Tracy Hickman—a book that sparked a lifelong love for dragons and epic quests.